ONE BABY STEP AT A TIME

BY
MEREDITH WEBBER

First published in Great Britain 2013
by Mills & Boon, an imprint of Harlequin (UK) Limited.
Harlequin (UK) Limited, Eton House, 18-24 Paradise Road,
Richmond, Surrey TW9 1SR

© Meredith Webber 2013

ISBN: 978 0 263 23480 0

Meredith Webber says of herself, 'Once I read an article which suggested that Mills & Boon were looking for new Medical Romance™ authors. I had one of those "I can do that" moments, and gave it a try. What began as a challenge has become an obsession— though I do temper the "butt on seat" career of writing with dirty but healthy outdoor pursuits, fossicking through the Australian Outback in search of gold or opals. Having had some success in all of these endeavours, I now consider I've found the perfect lifestyle.'

Recent titles by Meredith Webber:

CHRISTMAS WHERE SHE BELONGS
THE SHEIKH AND THE SURROGATE MUM
NEW DOC IN TOWN
ORPHAN UNDER THE CHRISTMAS TREE
MELTING THE ARGENTINE DOCTOR'S HEART
TAMING DR TEMPEST

**These books are also available in eBook format
from www.millsandboon.co.uk**

CHAPTER ONE

HE HADN'T EXPECTED it to feel so strange, walking into the ER at Willowby Hospital. After all, he'd been here often enough as a child—broken arm, a badly sprained ankle and, on one memorable occasion, suffering hypothermia after he'd been trapped down a well. Bill's fault, that! Bill crying pitiably at the top because her cat had fallen in—Bill going all girlie on him!

Whillimina Florence de Groote—his friend Bill!

Finally producing a daughter after six sons, Bill's mother had named her after both grandmothers, thinking it a nice feminine name, but from before she could talk, Bill had decided she was one of the boys and early on had insisted her name was Bill.

So Bill she'd stayed.

Lost in the past, he was startled when the woman who'd met him at the door—Lesley?—spoke.

'I'll introduce you to our senior nursing staff, and you'll meet the rest as you move around.'

But once again he was distracted, for there she was!

The wild, vivid, red hair, ruthlessly tamed for her work shift, burst like tendrils of flame from beneath her white cap, bringing smudges of colour to the sterility of the room.

'Bill!'

His delighted cry echoed around the still-quiet space and as he strode towards her, Lesley—he was sure it was Lesley—bleating, 'Oh, you know Bill?' as she followed him.

He watched as disbelief chased surprise across Bill's face, then delight dawned in a smile that made the brightly lit room seem even brighter.

'No one told me!' she said, abandoning the patient she'd been shepherding towards a cubicle to give him an all-enveloping hug. 'You didn't tell me you were coming,' she added, with a punch on his shoulder. 'But I'm so glad! Gran will be so happy. But what are you doing here? I'm working. Did you just call in to say hello?'

He grinned at her, the pleasure of seeing her again, from hearing the rush of words that was pure Bill, warming him right through.

'I'm working too,' he said, and saw shock dawn on her face.

'Working?'

He nodded.

'Here?'

He nodded again, still smiling broadly because he'd never seen Bill flabbergasted before, but flabbergasted she truly was.

'You've got a patient, I'll explain later,' he said, delighted that he could keep her guessing a while longer.

That drew a scowl but she did return to her patient, fully focussed on work once again, leaving Nick with a strange sense of... Well, he wasn't sure what it was— surely not *rightness* about returning home?

No, he was being fanciful. It was probably nothing more than the pleasure of seeing Bill again.

'You know Bill?' Lesley had been hovering behind him during the exchange.

'You could say that,' he replied, still smiling because somehow seeing Bill had made this decision to come home seem comfortable—even inevitable—for all he'd been thrown into work before he'd had time to settle in because of some emergency in the senior ER registrar's family.

Four hours later he'd had plenty of opportunities to see his old friend in action, her seniority evident in the way she designated duties and handled patients, always busy yet always calm and smiling.

Always attracting his attention whenever she was in sight, but that was nothing more than his natural delight in seeing her again. That she felt the same he had no doubt, for she'd flash a smile at him as their paths crossed.

Until now, when she was coming towards him with determination in her easy, long-legged stride, another scowl on her face.

'Tearoom *now*, Dr Grant!' she ordered, and he fell in obediently behind her, knowing he'd have a lot of explaining to do but pleased to have an opportunity to sit and talk to her in this small lull.

Had she ordered everyone out, that the area was empty? he wondered, as he followed her into the messy room. He wouldn't have put it past her, but right now he didn't care. All he wanted to do was give her a proper hug, to reaffirm he really *was* home again.

He caught her in his arms and swung her round, not easily as she was nearly as tall as he was—and only for a moment as she pushed away and glared at him.

'And what's all this about?' she demanded. 'Creeping into town without a word to anyone? And don't tell me Gran knows because I saw her yesterday and you know she can't keep a secret.'

He grinned at the red-headed termagant who'd bossed him around all his young life.

'Neither can you,' he reminded her, 'and I wanted it all settled before I told Gran. In the end, the job came up sooner than I expected so there was no time to tell anyone.'

Gold-brown eyes narrowed suspiciously.

'*What* is all settled?'

'The contract—twelve months with an option to extend.'

And now Bill was hugging him!

'Oh, Nick, Gran will be so happy. She never says anything but since that fall a month ago she's been feeling fragile and I think that makes her miss you more than ever. I can hear it in her voice when she talks about you.'

And you? Nick found himself wanting to ask, although why he wasn't sure. He and Bill had kept in close touch over the years, with regular emails and infrequent phone calls, very occasionally catching up in person when they'd both happened to be in the same city at the same time. It was what friends did so, yes, he did want her to be happy he was home...

'Sit, I'll make coffee,' Bill was saying, so he set the thought aside and sat, happy to watch her move around the little room, totally at home, composed—beautiful really, his Bill, although he'd probably always been too close to her to see it.

* * *

Bill shook her head as she set the kettle to boil, disbelief that Nick was actually here still rattling her thoughts. Her first glimpse of him had made her heart thud in her chest—just one big, heavy thud as she'd taken in the sight of the tall, lean man with a few threads of grey in the softly curling brown hair that had been the bane of his younger life. The black-rimmed glasses hid eyes she knew were grey-blue and gave him a serious look.

Her Nick, all grown up and devastatingly handsome now, she realised as she stepped back from their friendship and looked at him as a man.

They'd met in kindergarten class at Willowby West Primary School, a friendship begun when she had punched the boy who'd called Nick Four-Eyes. She'd dragged him home with her that afternoon, made him phone his gran to say where he was, then ordered a couple of her brothers to teach him how to fight.

And so the bond had been forged—a bond that had survived years of separation, though they'd always kept in touch and shared with each other what was happening in their lives.

Was there any tougher glue than friendship?

She found the tin of biscuits and put it on the table in front of him then brought their coffees over, setting them both down before plopping into the battered lounge chair opposite him, unable to stop staring at him and slightly embarrassed that he seemed to be equally focussed on her.

'Well?' she finally asked, mainly to break a silence that was becoming uncomfortable.

'It's been too long since we've seen each other,' he said. 'You've changed somehow.'

'It's been five years and then only for an hour at Sydney airport. Anyway, I never change, you should know that,' she teased. 'I was a skinny kid with wild red hair who grew into a skinny adult with wild red hair. But you, who knew you'd get so handsome?'

It was a weird conversation to be having with Nick—strained somehow. Although they'd gone in different directions after high school, he to Sydney to study medicine, she choosing Townsville for her nursing training, on other occasions when they'd caught up with each other, even briefly, they'd fallen back into their old patterns of friendship as if they'd never been parted.

Yet tonight was different.

'Will you stay with Gran?'

Gran was Nick's relation, not hers, but Bill was in the habit of calling in a couple of times a week, taking Gran shopping or getting library books for her.

With Nick here, Gran wouldn't need her...

'No, I spoke to Bob when the idea of the contract first came up. He offered me one of the penthouses at the new marina development he's just completed.'

'The sod!' Bill muttered, thinking of her eldest brother, the developer in the family. 'So *he* knew you were coming and said not a word to me! What's more, all I've got is a one-bedroomed apartment on the sixth floor in that building, and I bet he's giving you family discount as well.'

Nick smiled.

'But I am family, aren't I?' he retorted. 'I'm your seventh brother. Isn't that what you've always said?'

It was, of course, but it wasn't their relationship that was disturbing Bill right now, though what it was she couldn't pinpoint.

'It'll be a bit weird working with you,' she said, fairly hesitantly because that didn't seem to be what it was either.

Nick smiled and her heart gave another of those strange thuds.

'You only think that because you're used to being the one bossing me around and in the ER a doctor trumps a nurse.'

She rose to the challenge in his words.

'Oh, yeah? Says who?'

He didn't answer, just picked up his coffee, his smile still lingering about his lips, showing in fine lines down his cheeks and a crinkle at the corner of his eyes.

It was because she hadn't seen him for so long she had to keep staring at him, she was telling herself when the smile turned into a grimace.

'Aaargh! You call this coffee? You haven't heard of coffee machines? How backward *is* this place?'

Bill laughed.

'Not too backward these days but budget cuts are everywhere. You want fancy coffee you'll have to provide the machine and the beans, and everyone will use both and one night a junkie will steal the machine and you'll be back to instant.'

'I'll get a small one and lock it in my locker and it will be for my exclusive use,' Nick growled, sounding so like the old Nick of her childhood that Bill felt warmth spread through her.

This was going to be all right—wasn't it?

Bill was pondering this when Lesley burst through the door.

'Critical emergency on the way in, Dr Grant. Can you take the call from the ambulance?'

* * *

Forty minutes later Nick was ready—well, as ready as he would ever be. Although the town had grown, Willowby Hospital was still little more than a large country health centre. No specialist resuscitation area here, no emergency trauma surgeon on standby, just him and whatever nurses could be spared from the usual stream of patients on a Sunday night.

Him and Bill!

Right now she was setting up a series of trays on trolleys, IV and blood-drawing supplies, chest tubes, ventilator, defibrillator, medications, and was checking the supply of oxygen, the suction tubes, not fussing but moving with swift confidence and precision. Just watching her gave him added confidence about whatever lay ahead.

'The baler they spoke of—it's one of those things that rolls hay into huge round bales?' he asked, and she looked up from what she was doing to nod.

'Though what the lad was doing, putting his arm anywhere near the machine, is beyond me,' she said, before adding thoughtfully, 'I suppose if the string got caught you might think you could pull it loose and give it a tug. I've always thought night-harvesting had an element of danger because, unless you're used to night shifts, your mind might not be as sharp as it should be.'

Images of the damage such a machine could do to a human arm and shoulder flashed through Nick's mind, and he had to agree with Bill's opinion, but further speculation was brought to an end by the arrival of the ambulance and their patient, unstable from blood loss, his right arm loosely wrapped in now-bloody dressings, a tourniquet having been unable to stop the bleeding completely.

Nick listened as the paramedic explained what had been done so far—the patient intubated, fluid running into him, morphine to ease the pain, conscious but not really with them, so shocked it was clear the first-response team doubted he could be saved.

Hypovolaemic shock from loss of blood. The young man's heart would be racing, his hands and feet cold and clammy, his pulse weak—

'All we need to do is stabilise him enough for him to be airlifted down to Brisbane,' Bill reminded Nick, as if she'd heard the same thing in the paramedic's tone and had the same symptoms racing through *her* head.

So it began, the flurry of activity to keep the young man alive long enough for surgeons down south to save him. The paramedics had fluid flowing into him through his radial artery but he needed more.

While Bill hooked the patient up to the hospital's oxygen supply and monitors, taking blood to send to the lab for typing, Nick prepared to put a catheter into the left subclavian vein, anaesthetising the site, then advancing a needle carefully down beneath the clavicle, a guide wire following it when blood flowed freely into the needle's syringe.

Removing the needle, he made a small incision, his hands working mechanically while his mind raced ahead. Once the catheter, guided by the wire, was in place and more fluid was flowing in, he could examine the torn arm and shoulder in order to find the source of the blood loss.

'The tourniquet is holding back blood loss from the brachial artery,' Bill said, making Nick wonder if their childhood ability to follow each other's thoughts was still alive and well.

He looked across to where she was gently probing the damaged arm, flushing debris and carefully tweezing out bits of dirt and straw—the work a surgical assistant would be doing in a major trauma centre.

'I've been releasing the tourniquet and can see where the artery is damaged but he's so shocked I doubt that's the only source of blood loss.'

They were definitely following each other's thoughts!

He moved round the table, leaving another nurse to control the fluid while a third watched the monitors. He'd have liked to have an anaesthetist present, but that, too, was for city trauma centres, so he used a nerve block to anaesthetise the arm before examining it.

'There,' Bill said, passing him a loupe so he could see the torn artery more clearly.

Two tiny sutures and the tear was closed, but the nurse watching the monitors reported falling blood pressure.

Drastically falling blood pressure…

'V-tach,' the nurse said quietly.

The words were barely spoken before Bill had the defibrillator pushed up against the trolley and was already attaching leads to the paddles. Nick set the voltage, gave the order to clear, placed the paddles above and below the heart and watched as the patient's body jerked on the table.

He looked at the monitor and saw the nurse shake her head.

He upped the voltage, cleared again and felt the tension in the room as the body jerked and stilled, then the green line on the monitor showed the heartbeat had stabilised.

A release of held breath, nothing more than a sigh, but he knew everyone had been willing the lad to live.

For now!

'He's had three litres of fluid—he's definitely losing blood somewhere else,' he muttered, then turned to Bill. 'We need full blood—has he been cross-matched?'

'It's on its way,' she said quietly, then nodded towards the door where a young man in a white coat had appeared, stethoscope around his neck and, thank heavens, two blood packs in his hands.

'Rob Darwin, I'm one of two doctors on duty upstairs but Bill said you needed help down here, and when Bill calls, I obey. Her slightest wish is my command.'

He was joking, teasing Bill, but Nick had no time for jokes.

'Get that blood into him—it's warmed?'

Rob nodded and took up a position at the head of the table, fiddling with the fluid lines as he prepared to give the patient the transfusion.

'The bleeding has to be internal, but how? Where?'

Nick was talking to himself as he looked at the swollen, badly dislocated shoulder, picturing how the machine must have caught the arm and twisted it, trying to imagine where internal damage would have occurred.

'A tear to the axillary artery?' Bill suggested quietly, looking up from where she was putting clean dressings on the damaged arm.

'That or the subclavian,' Nick agreed. 'I'm going to have to go in and have a look.'

He glanced up at Rob.

'You okay with anaesthesia?'

Rob grinned.

'I haven't been here long but as Bill told me soon after I arrived, country doctors do the lot,' he said. 'How long would you want him out to it?'

'Hopefully twenty minutes, but double it—make it forty to be on the safe side. He's due to be flown out if we can get him stable.'

'The plane will wait,' Rob assured him, already checking the available drugs and drawing up what he'd need.

Bill prepared the area beneath where the young man's shoulder should be, quickly shaving the hair and swabbing antiseptic all around then stepping back as Nick made the incision.

'We know it's in the armpit—it should be right there,' Nick grumbled, but the muscle had been torn so badly it was hard to see where the armpit should have been.

A fresh flush of blood as Bill moved the lad's scapula revealed the tear, blood pulsing from it into the surrounding tissues.

'The pressure must have been enormous,' he murmured. 'It looks as if it's been ripped apart. I'll have to cut off the torn ends and sew it back together. The vascular surgeons in Brisbane can do the fancy stuff.'

Bill watched in utter amazement as the man she'd known so well as a boy—her first best friend—calmly performed life-saving microscopic surgery on their patient. But the whole shift had been one surprise after another, beginning with Nick walking into the ER as if he belonged there.

'Another suture!'

He snapped the order, making her realise he'd already asked while she'd been reliving the shock of his arrival. Her mind back in gear, she worked with him, actually thrilled to be seeing him in action—seeing just how good an emergency doctor he'd turned out to be.

Not that she'd ever doubted it. Nick had always been able to do anything, and even excel at it, once he'd set his mind to it.

Her friend Nick...

CHAPTER TWO

THE PATIENT WAS finally wheeled away, heading for an airlift to Brisbane and the experts who might or might not save his life and, with even more luck, his arm. Bill slid down the wall and slumped to the floor of the trauma room, oblivious to the mess of packaging, blood, swabs and tubing that littered the floor.

'Not bad for a first night on duty?' she said to Nick, smiling up at the man who leant against the wall across from her. 'Think you'll enjoy work back in the old home town?'

His face was drawn, the stress of the two-hour fight to keep the youngster alive imprinted clearly on his features, yet he found the shadow of a smile.

'Anything you can do I can do better,' he teased, using a phrase that had been bandied back and forth between them a thousand times in their youth.

A young nurse poked her head into the room.

'Want me to clean up?' she asked.

Bill shook her head.

'I'm off duty, I'll do it in a minute.'

She turned back to Nick to find him studying her, a strange expression on his face.

'What?' she asked, disturbed not by him looking at her but by her reaction to it—to him, the new him.

'Rob Darwin? Love interest?' he asked.

'As if!' Bill snorted. 'Not that he's not a nice young man, and not that he wouldn't like there to be something, but...'

She hesitated, finding her reluctance to date hard to put into words.

'No spark?'

Nick had found the words for her.

'None at all,' she said, 'and it seems a waste of my time and unfair to him just to date for the sake of dating.'

'Very noble of you,' he teased, then he smiled again.

This smile was better than the first one, and her reaction more intense.

Weird when this was Nick, but she didn't have time to consider it as he was speaking again and, anyway, maybe the reactions were nothing more than tiredness and the aftermath of stress.

'There must have been a spark with Nigel,' he was saying. 'What really happened there? You could have married him, the Great God of Surgery, and been taken away from all this. You could be down in the city, doing social stuff, running fundraising balls, lunching for good causes, decked out in designer gear instead of bloody scrubs.'

'Now, there would be a fate worse than death!'

The words were lightly spoken but pain pierced her heart as she remembered it had been that same 'Great God' who'd ordered her to have an abortion a month before their wedding because he didn't want people thinking they'd got married because she was pregnant.

She breathed deeply, aware that too much bitterness still leaked into her veins when she thought of that disastrous time.

The realisation that the man she'd loved had been nothing more than a shallow, social-climbing pretender had rocked her self-confidence and made her question her judgement about people, particularly men. The miscarriage two months later had exacerbated her loss of self-worth and it had taken years, back here in Willowby with her family and friends, to rebuild it.

Although now she'd grown a thicker skin and heavier armour to shield her fragile heart...

Nick heard the change in her voice and wondered how much damage her broken engagement had done to her trust—to Bill herself, given she was the most trusting person he had ever known. It worried him that he didn't know the background to the break-up—didn't know a lot of things about his friend.

His best friend!

What did the kids call it these days? BFF? Best friends for ever?

'Anyway,' she was saying, while his mind had drifted back to the past, 'if we're going to talk of what *might* have happened in our lives, *you* could have married Seraphina or whatever she called herself when *she* fell pregnant, and gone swanning off to New York to live off her earnings as a top supermodel.'

That was better, more like old times, Bill taking the fight to him!

'Serena,' Nick corrected. 'You're muddling her up with Delphina, who was the one before, and, anyway, I did offer to marry Serena but she wanted none of it, not me, not a child and definitely not marriage.'

Silence fell, the ghosts of dead children lying between them among the empty packaging and blood.

Bill reacted first, pushing herself up off the floor, stripping off her soiled apron and flinging it into a bin, then bending to begin collecting the rubbish off the floor.

'I'll do that.'

The young wardsman who appeared, mop and bucket in hand, waved her away and although she picked up a few more bits of rubbish, she was happy to leave him to it, following Nick out of the trauma room to find the big open area of the ER eerily quiet at six on a Monday morning.

'Everyone's sleeping in,' Andy, the duty ER manager, told them. Newly arrived on shift, he was spic and span, his face alert, his smile bright. 'Go home, both of you.'

'Got to dictate some notes on that last case,' Nick said.

'And I'm having a shower then heading for beach,' Bill told them. 'I need some sea air to clear my head before I can think about sleeping.'

Would she go to Woodchoppers? Nick wondered, not wanting to ask in front of Andy but aware he'd like to join Bill at the beach. Weird name for a beach, but it had been their favourite swimming beach growing up, Bill and her six brothers declaring it their personal fiefdom, keeping it free of any less desirable elements, particularly those pushing drugs to impressionable teenagers.

Whillimina de Groote and her brothers! They'd become the family he'd never had. Bill dragging him to her home after his first day at school, insisting her brothers teach the five-year-old Nick how to defend himself.

They'd taught him a lot after that...

* * *

Bill stood under the shower, the water so hot that steam was fogging the cubicle, but no amount of heat or water could wash away the uneasiness that lingered over her reaction to Nick.

To Nick as a *man*!

How pathetic!

She'd known him for close to thirty years, considered him her best friend in all the world, so why, now, would she be reacting to him as a man?

Maybe it was nothing more than the stress and tiredness engendered by their battle to save the teenager's life.

She could only hope…

Accepting that the hot water wasn't helping, she turned off the taps, dried herself hurriedly, rubbed at the tangled mess of red curls that topped her head and fell down past her shoulders, then pulled on an old bikini she kept in her locker, covered it with a voluminous T-shirt, grabbed her handbag and hurried out the staff exit, not wanting to bump into Nick before she'd had a good run on the beach and a swim in the limpid, tropical waters to clear her head.

Not before she happened to be on duty with him again, in fact, and if she spoke to the ER secretary who drew up the rosters, total avoidance might be possible.

Well, not total. He was back to see his gran, so they'd undoubtedly run into each other at Gran's house…

But at least he'd come home.

She pulled up in the small parking area at Woodchoppers Beach and slogged across the sand dunes, glad the effort of crossing them made the beach the least used of the beaches around Willowby. Pulling off her T-shirt and dropping it on the sand, she began to run, slowly at first then, as her muscles warmed, sprinting faster and faster—short sprints then slow jogs, alternating the two, feeling the blood surge through her body, bringing it to life in a most satisfactory manner.

Two more lengths of the beach and then she'd swim.

'You shouldn't come here on your own—you never know who might be around.'

Nick's appearance startled her.

'Obviously!' she snapped at him.

But as he ignored her comment and fell into stride beside her, she knew all the good of her run had vanished, and with it her peace of mind.

It's only Nick, she told herself, but that didn't seem to stop the awareness that prickled in her skin all down one side—the side closest to her jogging companion.

Veering away from him, she headed for the water and dived from ankle depth into the clear, green-blue sea, surfacing to breathe then diving again to porpoise along parallel to the beach, relishing the silken kiss of the water against her skin.

Had she always been this gorgeous?

Long, lean, and tanned in a way redheads weren't supposed to tan?

Nick watched as she dived and surfaced in the water, only to dive again, her limbs flashing in the sunlight, her hair trailing behind her—a mermaid at play.

Was it because she'd always been a friend that he'd never seen her as a woman? Not that he could afford to see her that way now—they were friends! There'd be plenty of interesting and intelligent, even beautiful, women here in Willowby. It was only a matter of connecting up with some of them, and the thoughts he found himself having about Bill would disappear.

For all she joked about having escaped a fate worse than death when she'd dumped Nigel, she was the kind of woman who should be married—married with a tribe of red-headed kids clustered around her—because she'd always been a mother hen, adopting not only him but any fellow pupil in danger of being bullied or excluded from one of the childhood gangs.

He stripped down to his jocks and dived into the water, surfacing a little distance from her, uncertain enough about the strange reactions of the night to not want to be too close.

'Race you to the rocks,' she challenged, and started immediately, but his longer strokes and stronger kick soon had him catching up, so they swam together towards the smooth, rounded rocks that jutted into the water at the end of the bay until they were close enough for him to swim away, beating her by a body length.

Strange reactions or not, he wasn't going to let her beat him!

'Oh, that was good,' she said, coming up out of the water, her hair streaming down her back. 'I find it's so much easier to sleep during the day if I have a run and a swim before I go home.'

She looked at him for a moment, her golden-brown eyes assessing.

'*And* a hearty breakfast at the surf club back at the main beach. You up for that, or has your body become a temple so you can't eat delicious crispy bacon, and beef sausages, and fried tomatoes, and all the other things that are loaded with cholesterol and fat?'

Nick shook his head in disbelief.

'So you still eat like a navvy and stay as slim as a whip. Some metabolism you de Grootes inherited.'

'Not all of us,' Bill told him, smiling as she waded in front of him back to the beach. 'Bob's developed a most unsightly paunch, and Joel's heading in the same direction. Too many business lunches and not enough exercise, that's the problem with those two.'

Nick watched the way her butt moved as she walked in front of him and tried to think of Bill's brothers rather than how those twin globes would fit into his hands.

'Have you already moved into the apartment?'

She threw the question over her shoulder but it brushed right past him, his attention snaffled by the way the woman in front of him moved, and how her breasts hung low as she bent to retrieve her T-shirt from the sand, the bikini she wore barely covering her nipples.

'Nick?'

Had she caught him watching her as she turned, her eyebrows raised as she waited for a reply?

What had she asked?

Had he moved in...?

'If you call dumping a couple of suitcases in the bedroom and unpacking my wash bag as moving in, then yes,' he responded, hoping the gap between the question and the answer hadn't been too long. 'It's fully furnished so all I had to bring were clothes and personal stuff. I'd hardly begun to unpack when the hospital phoned to ask if I could work last night.'

Bill didn't respond, so disturbed was she by the sight of Nick's lean, toned body that casual conversation was beyond her. He'd shrugged as he'd mentioned unpacking, an unfortunate movement as it had drawn her attention back to his chest, with its flat wedges of pectoral muscles and clearly defined six-pack.

She wanted to ask if he'd been working out, but that would give away the fact she'd noticed and the way she was feeling it was better if the question went unasked.

She climbed the first dune and raced down the other side then up the next, aware he was pacing himself to stay beside her—aware of *him*!

It was bad enough that he was living in the same building, so now she'd have to avoid seeing him out of work hours as well as at work, without him suspecting she might see him as other than a friend.

A passing fancy, surely?

But her reactions to him were forgotten as she topped the last dune.

'What is *that*?'

The words burst from her lips as she saw the racing-green sports car, hood down, cream leather seats, sleek lines shouting speed and, yes, seduction.

'My car?' His voice was quiet but she heard the pride in it.

'Well, *that* will get you noticed in Willowby,' she muttered, aware of just who would notice it first—the constant stream of beautiful women who used Willowby as a jumping-off place for reef adventures. True, they worked, if you could call hostessing on luxury yachts or on the six-star island resorts working, but since the mining boom had led to the town becoming one of the wealthiest per capita in the country, the place had been swamped by women, and men if she was honest, looking to separate some of that money from those who had it.

'Gets me noticed most places,' Nick replied, and the smile on his face made her stomach clench.

That's why he'd bought it! She knew that much immediately, remembering the email he'd sent her many years ago when he'd returned from his first stint with the army reserve, serving overseas. He'd helped to put back together young men blown apart by bombs in wars that ordinary people didn't understand.

He'd come home, he'd said, with one aim—to live for the day. He'd promised himself a beautiful car, the best of clothes and as many beautiful women as cared to play with him. 'I'm honest with them, Bill,' he'd said in the email. 'I tell them all it's not for ever, that marriage isn't in my long-term plans. You'd be surprised how many women are happy with that—even agreeing that it's not for them either. Things are different now.'

Were they? Bill hadn't been able to answer that question then and couldn't now. For herself, she knew she wanted marriage, and children too, but not without love and so far, apart from that one disastrous experience, love hadn't come along.

'Ride with me,' Nick suggested. 'I'll drop you back at your old bomb after breakfast.'

'Ride in that thing? The town might have grown, Nick, but at heart it's still the same old Willowby. I only need to be spotted by one of the local gossips and my reputation would be ruined. Did you see the de Groote girl, they'd be saying, running around in a fast car with a fast man? You, of course, will be forgiven. About you they'll say, hasn't he done well for himself, that grandson of old Mrs Grant? And such a kind boy, coming home to be with his gran now she's getting on.'

Nick laughed and headed for his car.

'Okay, but I won't offer to race you to the surf club,' he teased. 'Too unfair.'

Bill climbed into her battered old four-wheel drive, the vehicle her father had bought her new when she'd passed her driving test. She patted the dash to reassure the car she wasn't put off by its shabby appearance, or influenced by the shining beauty of Nick's vehicle, but it was she who needed reassurance as her folly in suggesting he breakfast with her finally struck home. Even with her sea-drenched curls, and the tatty old T-shirt, she'd always felt quite at home at the surf club, but these days many of the beautiful people breakfasted there as well—

Whoa! Surely she wasn't concerned that Nick would compare her to some of the other women and find her wanting?

Of course she wasn't!

Then why was she wondering if there might not be a long shift somewhere in the mess of clothes, books and papers in the back seat of the car—wondering if there might be a slightly melted tube of lip gloss in the glove box?

Hopeless, that's what she was.

He'd selected a table that looked out from a covered deck over the town's main beach and the placid tropical waters. Bill slipped into a chair beside him, so she, too, could look out to sea. Far out on the horizon they could see the shapes of the islands that dotted the coastline—tourist havens on Australia's biggest natural wonder, the Great Barrier Reef.

'I've ordered the big breakfast for both of us,' Nick

informed her. 'Anything you don't want, I'll eat. And coffee—double-shot latte still your drug of choice?'

'It is, and thanks,' Bill replied, telling herself at the same time that a nice normal breakfast with Nick should banish all the silly stuff that had been going on in her head.

Especially as Nick was wasting no time checking out the talent, with his eyes on a group of three long-haired blondes, laughing and joking on the other side of the wide deck.

'The town's scenery's improved,' he joked.

'It's the money that's being splashed around,' Bill reminded him, deciding to take his comment seriously. 'Money attracts money but it also attracts the kind of people who like to have it—like to spend it. The problem is that while the miners and the people who work in mining support services are all earning big money, the price of housing goes up, rents go up, and the ordinary people of the town, especially those who don't own their own houses, are stuck with costs they can't afford.'

Nick smiled.

'Still a worry-wart,' he teased.

'Well, someone has to worry about it. Nurses at the hospital don't get paid more than their counterparts in other places in the state, yet accommodation costs in town are enormous. Fortunately the hospital has re-alised it has a problem and has built some small rental apartments in the grounds, but you spread that problem out across the town—the check-out staff at supermarkets, the workers in government offices, the council truck drivers—all the locals suffer.'

She stopped, partly because she was aware she'd mounted her soap-box and really shouldn't be boring

Nick with the problem but also because the blondes appeared to have noticed him—new talent in town?—and were sending welcoming smiles his way.

'Maybe they saw the car when you drove in,' Bill muttered.

'Ouch! And anyway the car park's out the back. No, it's my good looks that have got their attention—see, one of them is coming over.'

One of them *was* coming over. The leggiest one, with the longest, shiniest, blondest, dead-straight hair!

'Aren't you Nick Grant?' she asked, and as Nick nodded, she held out her hand.

'I told the girls it was you. You used to go out with Serena Snow, didn't you?'

Again Nick had to agree, and the leggy blonde introduced herself.

'I'm Amy Wentworth. I met you a couple of times at parties back then. What are you doing up in this neck of the woods? Holidaying? Off to the reef for a few days' R and R?'

So far she'd totally ignored Bill—not that it mattered, Bill told herself.

She studied the woman while Nick explained he was working here, living in the new apartment building at the marina but with no elaboration on why. Amy raised her eyebrows.

'Can't imagine you in a hick town like this. Oh, I know there's a lot of money around, but what do you *do* when you're not working?'

Nick grinned at her.

'I'll be doing pretty much what I did when I wasn't working in Sydney.'

Amy drifted away but Bill wasn't going to let him get away with that tantalising reply.

'Which was?' she asked.

'What which was?'

'The "pretty much what you did in Sydney" bit of that conversation.'

'Ah, but I told you years ago,' he reminded her. 'I had a good time and I intend to do just that up here. You don't need nightclubs and friends with yachts on the harbour to have a good time.'

'We've got a nightclub and a two of my brothers have yachts, or big motor launches,' Bill said defensively, and Nick laughed.

'Exactly, although I think the nightclub crowd are a bit young for me, but you can have a good time wherever you are. In fact, I'm off for three days next week and think I might pop across to one of the island resorts—do a bit of diving and fishing and...'

'Meeting beautiful women,' Bill finished for him.

Again Nick smiled, although this time it was a little forced because in the back of his mind he'd had another reason for returning to Willowby, one that was becoming important to him.

'That too, of course,' he answered glibly. 'Want to come?'

CHAPTER THREE

SHE DIDN'T REPLY, studying him intently for a moment instead, and he knew that look. Undoubtedly she'd picked up something from his tone.

'Did it hurt you?' she asked.

Yep, he'd been right about the look and although he knew full well what she meant by the question, he wasn't going to cede ground to her by admitting it.

'Did what hurt me?'

'You know full well what I mean,' she said crossly. 'Serena saying no to your proposal.'

His turn to study her. The problem with friendship— a strong and enduring friendship like the one they shared—was that you couldn't lie to the other party. Oh, you could fudge around a bit and dodge answering, but you couldn't right out lie.

He turned his gaze from Bill's too-perceptive eyes and looked out over the beach and island-strewn sea.

The truth!

'More than I could have imagined,' he admitted, and turned back so, now it was out, he could meet the gold-brown eyes fastened so steadfastly on his face. 'I don't think it was Serena's rejection so much. I liked her well enough. For all her self-focus she was fun to be with

and happy that we more or less lived separate lives—
both of us working long hours at different times—so I
can't see why it wouldn't have worked.'

Bill's small, rather shocked 'Oh' broke into his
thoughts but now he'd started he wanted to finish what
he'd been saying.

'You know how I feel about the "l" word, Bill, so I
can't say I loved her, but what had…not excited but certainly intrigued me was the idea of having a family—
a wife and child—people who belonged, not to me but
with me, if you know what I mean.'

The disbelief on Bill's face was so easy to read he
had to laugh.

'Yes, yes, I know I said it would never happen,
but finding out Serena was pregnant, well, it kind of
changed something inside me, as if a wire that had
been shorted out was suddenly reconnected and family
stopped being in front of going down mines, abduction
by aliens and the bogeyman in my fears.'

He paused, marshalling his thoughts.

'In part, it's why I came home—came back to the
only family I've ever known: Gran and you de Grootes.'

'Looking for a family of your own?' Bill asked.

Again he paused, but honesty won out.

'Yes, I think so—I think it's what I need, Bill. What
I really want.'

'Oh, Nick,' Bill said softly, and she covered his hand
with hers as she had so often in the past. Though he'd re-
ciprocated often enough, when some fool of a youth had
hurt her in some way or when her pet hamster had died.

The strange thing was that this time it felt different.
Nice, but different.

'I also need to sleep,' he said, regaining control over

some erratic emotions and reclaiming his hand at the same time. 'Then this afternoon I must go over and see Gran. You want to come?'

Fool! Wasn't he going for distance here until he'd sorted out his reactions to his old friend?

'No, I saw her yesterday—well, the day before now—although,' Bill said firmly, 'that brings me to another issue. I had an email from you only last week—you answered the one I sent to say she was looking a whole lot better—and there wasn't a word about coming here to work. And if you were talking to Bob and pinching the best apartment in his building then you must have been fairly certain then.'

Nick laughed again—the disjointed sentence was sheer Bill, words tumbling over each other to get said, especially when she was angry with him.

'One,' he said, holding up his hand and pointing to his first finger, 'I wanted to surprise Gran and if I told you...'

He let the sentence hang but had the satisfaction of seeing a faint blush colour her cheeks. As honest as the day was long, Bill would be the first to admit she found it almost impossible to keep a secret.

'And two...' he pointed to his next finger '...I wasn't sure you were even here. In that email you'd said you had time off and were going to Townsville to talk to someone about some course.'

She nodded.

'The mine rescue people, about a new course. It *was* to be this week and next, but was cancelled. Pity really because it was going to be on flooded underground rescues and I haven't done that yet.'

'Mine rescue—flooded underground mines?' He

could hear his voice rising but couldn't stop it. 'What do you mean, you haven't done that yet? What on earth are you doing, getting involved with mine rescue, and what are your brothers doing, letting you do it?'

Her laugh made the sun seem brighter.

'Oh, Nick, you sound just like Bob, but Danny and Pete are already in the elite mine rescue squad and they've encouraged me to get involved. I'm not up to their standard yet—not flying off to foreign parts to help out—but I can hold my own as part of the local team when the experts are away, especially with my nursing and paramedic experience.'

Nick didn't know why he was surprised, but just the thought of mine rescue made him shudder. Danny, the second of the de Groote boys, had taken him and Bill down a mine when they'd been in their early teens, and though Bill had revelled in the darkness and gloom, he had hated every minute of the musty smell and the idea of being over a mile beneath the mountain.

Had been afraid every minute of it, to be honest, but he hadn't mentioned that part to his fearless friend.

Though Bill was terrified of snakes, so—

'I'm heading home to bed,' she said, cutting into his thoughts and sounding so casually at ease she obviously wasn't feeling any of the strangeness he was. 'I guess I'll be seeing you around.'

She stood up, paused, then dropped a light kiss on the top of his head.

'Nice to have you back, curly,' she added lightly, before weaving her way between the tables and disappearing round the corner of the deck.

He couldn't help but turn and watch her go.

* * *

Bill pondered Nick's startling revelation that he'd discovered he wanted a family. Was that why he'd come home? Did he see Willowby as the place to raise this family?

They were unanswerable questions so she moved on to considering the uneasiness the subject had caused in her insides when it was nothing at all to do with her.

Although hadn't that been *her* dream? The memory of her delight in finding she was pregnant made her stomach tighten.

Enough!

No melancholy!

And anyway, wasn't there enough to occupy her brain with Nick's sudden reappearance?

She drove home slowly and carefully, aware she was tired, but her mind now snagged on the unexpectedness of the situation—on Nick.

But thinking about it, she could see it was only natural that Nick *would* want a family for all he'd spent his youth mocking the institution. She'd always known his mockery was to cover the hurt of his own parents' behaviour, jaunting around the world, crewing on luxury yachts, visiting exotic places, their son left with his grandmother not, as they'd said, so he'd have stability but because it had made it easier for them to continue to enjoy their lifestyle.

They'd eventually drowned at sea when their own, much smaller yacht was caught up in a typhoon, but their deaths had had little effect on Nick because Gran had given him more than stability, she'd given him love—unquestioning and all-encompassing love.

So, while Nick's admission was surprising, it was

her own reaction to it that needed more consideration. As did her reaction to the sight of his bare chest, and the way his muscled thighs had matched her strides on the beach, or the strange feelings seeing him had produced, not in her heart where their friendship lived, but along her nerves and—

No, she wasn't going there!

Surprise—that's what had caused the weird reactions.

She stopped at the control panel to the underground parking area to press in the security code then drove in as the big door opened. She parked and made her way to the lift, the exhaustion that followed a busy night on duty fast catching up with her.

Exiting on the sixth floor, she headed down the corridor to her apartment, an end one with a view out to sea, a really special place to live for all she'd complained about its size. Two floors above her the two penthouses spread across the top level—big four-bedroom homes, each with three bathrooms, wide decks taking in the view out over the Coral Sea, and a smaller deck on the western side, looking back towards the green-clad mountains.

Bill smiled to herself, pleased that even in choosing accommodation that might only be for a year, Nick was following his avowed intention to have nothing but the best!

It had to be tiredness, Nick decided as he drove home, that had weakened him to the extent he'd admitted his disappointment over Serena and the baby to Bill. Normally he'd have teased her about being nosy, or asked a question about her own love life to divert her attention from the fact he hadn't answered, but, no, he'd heard himself bleating out his pathetic reaction, even feeling remembered pain for the loss of a dream—a family of his own.

But he *hadn't* lost the dream, he reminded himself. Wasn't that why he was here? He'd been drawn back by Gran, of course, but also by the feeling that in Willowby he might find the woman who would help the dream come true. A family woman and, yes, his thinking had been that Bill would know someone who'd be just right for him—Bill or someone in *her* family. They were into family in a big way, the de Grootes.

And hadn't he always turned to Bill when he had a problem, or needed help?

Letting himself into the penthouse, he set aside his tumbling thoughts and sighed with pleasure. The familiar view out across the island-dotted sea still took his breath away. And tired though he was, a part of him wanting nothing more than to slip into bed, he had to walk out onto the balcony and breathe in the fresh sea air.

He was home.

Second night on duty. No life-threatening emergencies and he'd heard from the hospital in Brisbane that his patient from the previous night was doing well.

'It has to be the night for the bizarre,' Bill said, slumping down beside him in the tea room during a lull in proceedings. 'I suppose dog bites are common enough, but the bite usually doesn't come with a couple of dog teeth in the wounds. The dog must have been a hundred and five for its teeth to have come out so easily.'

Nick shook his head.

'I can't believe I nearly missed the second one. It was weird enough discovering one tooth in a puncture wound, but it was only when you were putting on the dressing that I realised I hadn't probed the second hole and, sure enough, another tooth.'

'Perhaps someone wrenched the dog off and that's why it lost the teeth.'

Nick considered this for a moment.

'No, there'd have been tearing around the wounds and there was no sign of that—just bite holes and teeth.'

'From an ancient dog or one with a gum problem.'

'And the kid with his head stuck in the bars of his cot,' Nick recalled. 'You'd have thought his father would have had a hacksaw to cut through a bar and release him instead of taking the cot to pieces to bring it in for us to do it.'

'It did look funny.' Bill smiled at the memory of the two parents arriving with the side of the cot held between them, and the grandmother carrying the perfectly contented baby, which had been looking around with wide-eyed curiosity and doubtless wondering about all the fuss.

'Cute baby, though,' Bill added, although she knew she should dodge baby conversations altogether because even after more than a year it hurt to see other people's babies.

'Very cute,' Nick agreed, rising to his feet as his pager buzzed.

'Drunk in cubicle three,' the duty manager told Bill as she returned to work. 'There's a nurse in there with Nick but they might need more help.'

Bill closed her eyes for a moment. Babies were upsetting enough, but if there was one thing she hated, it was handling drunks. They came in all shapes and sizes, and varied from angry and abusive, through straight obstreperous, to wildly happy, laughing hilariously as they threw up on your uniform and shoes.

'Obstreperous,' Nick said under his breath as Bill entered the cubicle. 'He's had a fall, I'd say into a bougainvillea as he has multiple abrasions, a dislocated finger and some very nasty thorns sticking out of his legs.'

The man in question was insisting he was perfectly all right, if Bill was translating his drunk speech correctly, but whenever he moved on the examination table the thorns dug in and he'd yelp with pain.

'I'm going to give him a local anaesthetic then fix the finger,' Nick continued. 'If you two can hold him still for a minute, I'd be grateful.'

The finger joint went back into place, and the young nurse cleaned and bandaged the man's hand so the finger would be supported while the joint healed.

'We'll start on the thorns,' Nick told Bill, but it was easier said than done when the man kept insisting he was fine and trying to climb off the table.

'Who brought him in?' Nick asked the young nurse.

'His wife. She's out in the waiting area.'

'Could you ask her to come in?' Nick smiled as he made the request and Bill couldn't help but notice the nurse's blush.

Still winning women over wherever he goes, she thought, but though she'd thought it a thousand times before, this time it didn't prompt a smile.

'Being a nuisance, is he?' the woman who entered demanded, before turning to her husband. 'Now, listen, you, sit still and let the doctor do his job or I'll take you home and throw you back into the bougainvillea my-self, and don't think I wouldn't do it.'

The man on the table quietened immediately and looking from him, a bulky six-footer, to the small slim wife, Bill had to smile.

'Thank you, madam.' Nick gave the wife a small bow. 'It's good to know who's the boss in the house-hold.'

She smiled at Nick.

'It probably wouldn't work if he was a habitual drunk, but as it is, he can't hold his grog so mostly he doesn't drink, but we've just had our first grandchild and he went out with his mates to wet the baby's head—they insisted, and now look at him. Fine example for the kid he'll be!'

She spoke fondly and even smiled at her husband, settling into a chair beside the wall to make sure he behaved.

Bill worked beside Nick, swabbing each scratch and wound as he pulled out the thorns.

'I can do this,' she said to him, but he shrugged away her offer and continued working until they had the now sleeping drunk patched up and able to be released to his wife.

'Just watch the wounds in case they begin to fester. There's no point starting antibiotics if he doesn't need them, but come back or go to see your own GP if they worry him,' Nick told her as he helped her take the man out to the waiting room where an aide would help her out to the car.

'Babies do keep cropping up,' he said to Bill as she came out of the cubicle, a bag of debris in her hand.

I'm glad he said that, Bill decided, setting aside her

own feelings and thinking just of Nick. It must mean he's over or getting over the loss of what he'd thought would be his very own family.

'Some nights are like that,' she reminded him. 'I'd far prefer a run of babies, as long as they're not too sick, to a run of drunks.'

'Hear, hear!'

This from the nurse who had followed Bill out of the cubicle, although she'd spoken to Nick rather than Bill. The nurse was from an agency—distinctive in the agency uniform—someone Bill didn't know. But studying her now, as the nurse continued to chat to Nick, Bill realised she was exactly his type—tall, curvy, blonde.

And, no, that wasn't a stab of jealousy. Her and Nick's friendship had survived a long stream of blondes, some, like Serena, Bill had seen in photos, and some she'd only heard about through emails and texts.

The agency nurse was now suggesting she and Nick have a coffee and as the ER was virtually deserted, it was only natural he should accept, although he did turn his head to ask, 'Want another coffee, Bill?'

Bill shook her head and headed off to dispose of the rubbish, hearing the agency nurse question the name Bill and Nick explaining.

This had to stop! she told herself as she hurled the bag of rubbish down the chute. Her friendship with Nick had survived because neither of them had ever had the slightest interest in the other in a romantic way. Growing up, she'd have as soon considered falling in love with one of her brothers.

It had to be that she hadn't seen him for so long that she was suddenly seeing him as a man.

Reacting to him as a man!

When *had* she last seen him?

He'd been in New York, proposing to Serena, when she'd broken off her engagement to Nigel, and although Nick had promised faithfully he'd be home for her wedding, once that was off, he'd headed for foreign parts, doing his bit for the army once again.

Oh!

It all fell into place now. There'd been no mention of a second deployment overseas prior to all that happening, but obviously he'd been sufficiently upset to want to get as far away as possible from everyone and everything.

Poor Nick!

Nick chatted to the nurse—Amanda—and wondered why Bill hadn't joined them.

Not that it mattered. Amanda was amusing and obviously happy to keep both sides of the conversation going so he could brood a little over the reactions he was feeling towards Bill.

Physical reactions!

Disturbing, because at the same time it felt a little like incest—this was Bill, his friend…

'So, you'll come?' he heard Amanda ask.

Unwilling to admit he had no idea what she was talking about, he said, 'Of course!'

'Great. The boat will leave from the City Marina, gangway four, at ten.'

'Ten today?' Dead giveaway, that question, but it had just burst out.

'No, Saturday, silly,' Amanda said, giggling and cuffing him lightly on the arm, moving close enough

on the settee for him to know he should have been following the conversation.

Oh, well, some time between now and Saturday he'd
have to sort out an excuse. Except going out on a boat
with Amanda, and presumably her friends, might get
his mind off Bill.

And wasn't he here to meet women—maybe the one
woman with whom he could plan his family?

The shift ended and he was pleased to see Bill's age-
ing car still in the car park. He wouldn't be tempted to
follow her to the beach, which was good as he didn't
think his libido could handle the sight of her in a bikini
again. Not just yet, anyway.

Perhaps after Saturday…

Tired enough to sleep without the swim and run on
the beach, he drove to his apartment, pulling up at the
security panel at the entrance to the building's basement, staring in shock at what looked like a derelict's
collection of junk on the footpath beside the big doors.

Except it wasn't a derelict but Serena rising from
the pile of belongings. Serena with a doll in her arms.

Obviously he was losing his mind—hallucinating…

What drugs had he handled during the night?

Shock had him riveted to his seat as the mirage that
possibly *was* Serena walked towards the car. Now he
could hear the words she was saying clearly enough,
he just couldn't make sense of them.

'Came in on an early flight, no one answering the
bell, thought you'd be home eventually, and as you'd
never walk if you can drive, I thought this was the best
place to catch you, but now you're here I really need
to hand Steffi and all her gear over, and I'm terribly
sorry to do this, Nick, I really am, and I know you're

going to be mad as hell, and I'll explain when we get to your apartment, but we'll have to hurry because I'm booked to fly out again at midday to catch the evening flight to New York.'

New York!

It was in New York he'd last seen Serena, heard her tell him she didn't want a baby, yet here she was, not with a doll but a baby in her arms...

He leapt out of the car, straight over the door, looming over her.

'What will you explain?' he roared.

Then a voice behind him said, 'Hush, Nick, you'll upset the baby.'

Bill!

Unable to get into the car park with him blocking the road, she must have pulled up behind him and got out to see what was happening.

'You must be Serena,' she added politely, and he remembered sending Bill a glamour shot of Serena some years before. 'You don't know me but I'm Nick's friend Bill. We grew up together and now we both live in this apartment block my brother built. And as our cars are blocking the entrance, what if we put all the gear into my car and you and the baby get in with Nick and we'll get the stuff up to his apartment and the two of you can take it from there?'

Nick watched in total bemusement as Bill efficiently loaded what looked like a truckload of baby paraphernalia into her car and Serena, plus baby, slid into his.

'Drive through!' Bill ordered, and he recovered sufficient composure to do as she told him, sliding the car into his parking space and watching as Bill stopped beside the lift and unloaded Serena's belongings.

But Serena was flying to New York this evening—so why had she flown a couple of thousand miles north to leave the stuff here?

And the baby?

No, he couldn't think about the baby.

By now Serena had joined Bill at the lift and together they were stacking the gear inside, Bill's voice echoed around the basement—Bill's voice finally bringing him out of his daze.

'You're saying this little girl is Nick's baby?' Bill's outrage was clear and the words sank through his bewildered brain.

This is where you get out of the car and demand an explanation, Nick told himself, but his legs had turned to jelly.

He had a child.

A daughter!

Nick saw Bill take the baby and turn his way. She obviously felt it was time he emerged from his car and took control of the situation.

Would his legs work?

Of course they would.

He had a child—

He leapt out of the car.

'This is *my* baby?' he demanded, coming close to Serena and echoing Bill's words. 'You didn't have an abortion and you didn't bother telling me? Why would you do that? And now what? You've decided kids are more trouble than they're worth and you want to hand her over, as if she's a bit of furniture you no longer need?'

Bill had moved a little away, cradling the little head

protectively against her chest, one hand over the baby's other ear so it couldn't hear him yelling at its mother.

'Look,' Serena muttered, holding up her hand as if she needed to ward off further attack. 'I know this is inconvenient, Nick. When I had the baby Mum looked after her, with nannies to help out, but Mum's just got married again and I've got this huge offer for a special show in New York and Mum had a nanny lined up— Mum always vetted the nannies—but the nanny walked out and so I thought, well, it's not as if you haven't got family up there—with Gran and all those de Grootes you talk about all the time—you'll find someone to take care of her.

'She's a good little thing and she's used to strangers minding her and she's been to day care as well. I've brought all her things and the last nanny wrote down her schedule so I'm sure with a bit of help you can sort things out.'

At least Serena was right about family. At last count Bill had about twenty-two nieces and nephews, so someone in the family would be happy to take care of one more baby.

The thought brought anger in its train—a hot, deep, burning fury!

'I can't believe that even you—' he began, before Bill arrived and put her hand on his chest, pushing him back a step.

'You cannot murder her here—not in front of Steffi,' she said firmly. 'Besides, don't you think it's time you met your family?'

Bill's smile was forced but it worked, dousing his anger just a little, and when she put the little curly-haired girl into his arms it disappeared altogether.

Bill said, 'Steffi, meet your daddy.'

And Nick understood that love wasn't something you could explain or analyse, it was something you felt...

CHAPTER FOUR

NOW HE TOOK control of the situation, ordering—yes, it definitely was an order—the two women to take the stuff up to his apartment.

'And you'll be?' Serena demanded huffily.

'Coming in the next lift—I'm certainly not going to overload it with a baby in my arms.'

And with that he turned his back on them and looked down at the warm scrap of humanity snuggled against his chest.

He had a baby!

Or did he?

Serena had been adamant about the abortion, so was this little girl really his?

He held her out and had to smile. A fluff of soft brown curls, wide blue eyes—Gran's eyes—and a dimple, now she smiled at him, in her left cheek, just where his annoying dimple was.

His heart jolted in his chest then hammered furiously and he held the baby close again because he knew he was shaking with the sheer enormity of this revelation.

He pressed kisses on her head and murmured nothings until his heart resumed its normal beat and he felt confident enough to hold her out again and look into her face.

'Hi, there,' he said softly. 'I'm your dad!'

Serious eyes studied him, taking him in.

Judging him?

No smile, but who could blame her?

'We'll be all right,' he assured her, and hugged her closer.

The lift returned and he got in, taking it to the top floor and striding out, ready to face whatever lay ahead, but knowing, already, that the baby was here to stay.

Bill had heard the word 'besotted', and probably even used it herself to describe a teenager's crush, but she'd never seen besotting happen—not as quickly and completely as it must have happened for Nick to walk into the apartment looking as he did.

Oh, dear, she thought, absolutely thrilled for Nick but worried over what might lie ahead.

She'd helped Serena take all Steffi's belongings up to Nick's penthouse, mentally listing all the things he'd need if he intended keeping the baby here—a cot to begin with and probably a playpen so she'd be safe if he was called to the phone.

Baby bath?

'Bill?'

Nick's voice brought her out of her mental listing.

'I asked if you'd mind taking Steffi down to your place for half an hour while I have a talk to Serena?'

Bill smiled as she took the baby, although the smile was forced.

But this was for Nick and she was pleased he didn't want the little one to hear her parents yelling at each other, because some yelling was sure to happen, although as ever when she held a baby she had very mixed emotions—reminders of what might have been.

Could babies feel doubt and uncertainty churning in the breast that held them?

Just in case they could, she pulled herself together and made a special effort, smiling at the little girl and talking gently.

'So, Steffi,' she said as they went down to her apartment, 'you're, what? Nearly a year old? Ten months? You're gorgeous, do you know that?'

The little girl smiled and that was it for Bill as well—besotted!

Oh, dear.

Falling in love with this particular baby would *not* be a good idea. This was Nick's family, not hers.

She'd expected Nick to phone so the knock on the door when she'd just got Steffi to sleep on cushions on the floor surprised her.

'I had to phone Bob to find out where you lived,' Nick said, running his hand distractedly through his hair. 'You've no idea, Bill, you just won't believe it. Where is she? Steffi?'

Bill led him inside, pointed to the sleeping child, then took him through to the kitchen for coffee.

'Sit,' she ordered, 'and drink this before we start.'

She handed him a fresh coffee, made one for herself, then sat opposite him at the breakfast bar.

'So?'

Nick was still shaking his head, and she understood the depth of his disbelief when he began.

'Having told me she'd have the abortion, she goes

to stay with Alex, the Russian photographer who worships the ground she walks on, and he throws up his hands in horror, not at her destroying a human life but because this is the photographic opportunity of a lifetime, something he's always dreamt of doing, and here's his favourite subject, his muse, presenting him with the opportunity!'

'What is?' Bill asked, totally bewildered.

'Well you might ask,' Nick growled. 'A coffee-table book detailing nine months of pregnancy—well, seven and a half months, in actual fact. Nude photos of Serena in all poses, in all lights, the bulge growing ever larger. Imagine how Steffi's going to feel about *that* when she's growing up.'

Bill had to laugh.

'Right now I think you have more to worry about than what Steffi's going to think as a teenager. Why didn't Serena tell you she'd changed her mind and was going ahead? You'd offered to marry her—you wanted a family.'

Nick groaned.

'Yes, I had and, yes, I did, but she really didn't want to be married, and apparently my talk of family had frightened her because it was the last thing *she* wanted. A family would tie her down and she needed to be free to pursue her career. I know that makes hers sound cold and uncaring, but she isn't really, she's just got the most total self-focus of anyone I've ever met.'

'So what was she thinking, going ahead with the pregnancy?' Bill demanded, wondering where uncaring finished and self-focus began.

'Oh, that's easy. You have to remember that Serena thinks differently to ninety-nine per cent of the human race and it turned out she knew this wonderful couple in New York who wanted to adopt so she knew the child would go to a good home, and she could keep in touch as a kind of surrogate aunt.

'*Only* Serena could think something like that was okay. The woman has a warped mind—I always knew that, even when I was going out with her. Her career is the be-all and end-all of her life, and everything else, even romance, is incidental. I blame her mother, who had Serena appearing in ads from the time she was born, but as an adult Serena's had choices and the number-one choice has always been her career.'

The disbelief and despair in Nick's voice shocked Bill so much she came round to give him a hug.

'It's okay. For whatever reason, she did keep the child, and Steffi's here.'

'It's not okay!' Nick roared, then turned quickly to see if he'd woken his daughter, and quietened his voice when he added, 'The only reason she didn't give *my* daughter up for adoption—apparently that old goat Alex had intended putting his name down as the father for adoption purposes—was that he suddenly decided he could document the child's life as well, but, you know what, once she grew from a swaddled bundle to a chubby six-month-old, she *wasn't photogenic!*'

Nick was right, the behaviour of two so-called adults defied belief, and he had every right to the anger she could feel in the tight muscles and sinews of his body.

'So, Steffi's now surplus to requirements,' Bill muttered, as a murderous rage began to build inside *her.*

'Well, not entirely. I think Serena, in her own way, probably loves her, and Serena's mother was always around, but who knows what would have happened to

Steffi if that Amy woman hadn't seen us at breakfast yesterday and phoned Serena, whose pea-brain immediately came up with a solution to the dilemma of this offer in New York right when her mother's off on a honeymoon, and whatever nanny she had decided to leave at a moment's notice. Give Steffi to her daddy for a while!'

'For a while?' Bill repeated.

Nick looked at her and shook his head.

'Apparently we can "talk"—Serena waggled her fingers in that silly way to make the inverted commas— when she comes home. *I'll* say we'll talk!'

'Let's worry about that later,' Bill suggested, hearing the exhaustion beneath the anger in Nick's voice and hugging him again. 'Now, at least, Steffi's landed in a proper family, with you to love her, and Gran, and me, and twenty-two kind-of cousins, and a plethora of aunts and uncles. All we have to do is sort out how to manage.'

'Manage?' Nick repeated, looking up at her as she went back round the bar and resumed her stool, aware that hugging Nick was *not* a good idea, no matter how badly he had needed to be hugged.

'Nick, you have a baby and you work and the ER at the local hospital isn't the kind of place where you can take your baby to work.'

He turned to look at his sleeping child and the expression in his eyes caused a stab of pain in Bill's chest.

'I work nights,' he said softly. 'I don't suppose there's such a thing as night care.'

Bill saw the complexity—the enormity—of the situation dawn on his face so wasn't surprised when he turned to her, anguish in his voice.

'What will I do, Bill? How can I manage?'

With a great deal of difficulty, Bill thought, but she didn't say it. The poor man was bamboozled enough as it was.

'*We'll* manage,' she said firmly. 'Serena was right about one thing. While Gran might be a bit beyond minding a baby full time, you've a whole herd of de Grootes out there who'll be only too willing to help. But first you have to decide just what help you want.

'Full time, part time? I know you've just started a new job, but there's such a thing as paternity leave. We can make some temporary caring arrangements until the hospital replaces you, if you want to be a full-time dad for a while so you and Steffi can get to know each other. Then there are well-trained nannies you can get, even in Willowby, again either full time or part time, live-in or daily, and they can be contracted short or long term.'

He stared at her and she knew he hadn't taken in much of what she'd said, his mind still reeling from shock and disbelief.

'You're exhausted. Give me your keys then go into my bedroom and go to sleep. When Steffi wakes I'll take her back upstairs and get things set up for her there.'

Oh!

'You do intend she lives with you?'

That woke him out of his daze.

'Where else would she live?' he demanded.

'Good! Now go to bed?'

It had to be a measure of his shocked state that he obediently handed over his keys and went into her bedroom, shutting the door behind him, no doubt so she wouldn't see him slump onto the bed and bury his head in his hands as he tried to come to grips with this massive change in his life.

A measure of his state that he didn't argue that she, too, needed to sleep, but Bill knew it would be easier for the hospital to find another nurse to take her night shift tonight than it would be to find another doctor.

Bill looked towards the closed door. In her heart she knew she should be getting less involved with this child, not more, but Nick was in trouble and she'd reacted automatically—helping out in times of trouble was what they'd always done for each other.

Nick sat on Bill's bed, head bowed, his fingers running through his hair as if rubbing at his scalp might stimulate his thinking.

What thinking?

His brain was numb!

He had a daughter?

What was he going to do?

How could he look after her even for a short time?

What did he know about bringing up children?

He didn't even know her birthday...

He gave a despairing groan and slumped back on the bed, surprised to find that he might actually go to sleep.

His body handling stress by shutting down his mind, the doctor in him suggested as he drifted off.

He woke mid-afternoon to find a note from Bill beside the bed.

We're at your place, here's a key.

'We're at your place...' he read again, this time aloud, and felt dread and panic surging in his stomach.

What should he do?

What *could* he do?

But even as he asked himself the question he remembered the feel of that little body against his chest and he headed into Bill's bathroom, took a shower, used her far-from-adequate razor to scrape stubble from his cheeks, then, clad in a rather ragged towelling robe he found behind the bathroom door, he grabbed his dirty clothes, and the key, and headed up to his apartment.

Except it wasn't his apartment, it was a nursery school. Colourful toys and strange objects were strewn around the place, and in the midst of this chaos a small person stood, holding onto his glass-topped coffee table—he'd have to get rid of that—and waving a chubby hand in his direction.

'Hey,' he said quietly, squatting down—not easy to do decently in the robe—and moving carefully towards her. 'How are you, Steffi? How are you, little girl?'

Wide-set eyes studied him intently, the little face serious as she took in the stranger talking to her. Then one chubby hand reached out for his and as he took it he felt his heart breaking right in two. Suddenly she let go of the coffee table and with grin as wide as the universe she toddled towards him, her delight in her forward progress bringing a gurgle of laughter as well as the smile.

He caught her as she toppled, and sat on the floor with her in his arms, picking up a floppy doll and making it dance in front of her.

But she was more interested in him, probing at his glasses, studying his face again, touching his hair, his ear, his lips until he felt his chest would burst with the love blossoming inside it, and he knew tears were form-ing in his eyes.

Bill must have been watching from a distance be-cause as Steffi's crawled off his knee to stand up at the glass table again to practise her walking, Bill came in and sat down on the sofa, waving her hand at the chaos around them.

'I'm sorry about all this,' she said, 'but you know the de Grootes, competitive to a man—or woman in this case. I phoned Bob's wife to ask about a cot and a high chair and next thing I knew every one of the sisters-in-law had turned up, all bringing something for Steffi. You should see the bedroom. As well as the cot you have chests of drawers, colourful mobiles, pictures on the wall, a change table and some kind of bin that wraps up dirty nappies. That is, of course, if you're going to use disposables, which are a lot more eco-friendly now.'

For about the fortieth time today Nick was dumb-founded.

'Disposable nappies? I have to make decisions about things like that?'

Bill laughed.

'About a lot of things, Daddio!' she teased. 'There's home-cooked or scientifically balanced bottled food, there are about ten different kinds of baby formula and you have to choose one, there's how early to start swim-ming lessons, there's day care or a nanny, which kindy to put her name down for, which school will she go to, how young's too young to have boyfriends—'

'Okay!' Nick said, and as he held his hand up to stop Bill's teasing, Steffi grabbed it as support and again walked towards him, collapsing happily into a giggling heap on his lap.

He was in love!

'From a purely practical point of view,' Bill continued, 'I've told the hospital I won't be in for a week and can mind her while you're at work and when you're sleeping during the day. She's so good about going down for a nap—on the cushions at my place and in a totally strange cot—I think she's used to being passed around to different carers—but I think it would be best if she gets settled into her bedroom so, if it's okay with you, I'll sleep over here until you're sorted.'

'Okay with me? Until I'm sorted?'

Nick rested his chin on his daughter's curly hair and looked up at his friend, and smiled.

'You realise that might be never,' he warned, 'the sorted bit. And when did we ever have to ask about staying over at each other's places?'

He looked around at all she'd achieved while he'd slept, and added, 'Thank you, Bill, from the bottom of my heart. I was in such a blind panic I had no idea where to turn or what to do, and you've calmly worked everything out—made it easy for me. I owe you, big time!'

Bill smiled at him, but he thought he saw a hint of sadness in the smile.

The broken engagement? Had *she* been looking forward to a baby of her own?

In which case was this fair, relying so much on her to be Steffi's carer while he worked things out?

'Well, now you're up and about, I'll introduce you to your new belongings—the physical ones.' Bill's voice was carefully neutral, nothing to read there, so maybe he'd imagined the sadness. 'You can bring Steffi,' Bill continued, 'because learning to do things with her on one arm is all part of fatherhood training.'

Which was all very well but how did he stand up with a baby in his arms? What if he fell?

He solved this dilemma by putting Steffi on the floor, standing up then lifting her, although he knew full well he *could* have performed the feat with her still in his arms. In the kitchen he was introduced to bottles, formula, baby food in small jars, yoghurt in the refrigerator, a sterilising machine that would have held its own in a hospital, bibs, baby bowls, baby spoons, baby cereal.

He took it all in, realising it was far less complicated than it had seemed at first glance, but it was Bill's attitude that was bothering him. Nothing overt, nothing he could put a name to, but it seemed as if she was distancing herself from him.

From him or from Steffi?

The Bill he remembered had been passionate about small children, babysitting all through their teenage years, so while he wasn't actually doing her a favour by letting her mind Steffi while he got sorted, he'd have thought she wouldn't mind. And, after all, she'd suggested it!

But there was something off—something too matter-of-fact in all this—

'Are you listening?' the person he was worrying about demanded.

'Boiled water,' he repeated diligently, then had to admit, 'No, I wasn't. What do I do with boiled water?'

Bill frowned at him.

'According to the notes, you still have to boil the water to mix with her formula for her bottles and she has three a day, one before each nap and one before bed.

She's got to be, what, eleven months old, so I would have thought maybe by now ordinary water would do, but I've written Kirsten's number on the notes, she's Andre's wife and the most sensible of my sisters-in-law and won't talk on for ever if you ring to ask her something.'

Nick looked at the notes, then back at Bill, thinking of the expression he thought he'd seen on her face— thinking too that, with the other strange stuff happening when he was around Bill, he should be seeing less, not more of her.

'Are you sure you want to take this on?' he asked. 'After all, I *could* just tell the hospital I can't work for a while, they'd battle on, and once I've read the notes, how hard can it be?'

She shook her head.

'You'll soon find out. I'm going to have a sleep, but I'll be up before you go to work. You can organise whatever you like with the hospital once you've thought it through.'

She tapped the notes to remind him to read them, and departed, leaving his bunch of keys and taking the single spare he'd used when he'd come up from her apartment.

And, despite the warm body he held in his arms, the place felt cold now Bill had gone...

Exhaustion hit Bill as she left the apartment, tiredness so strong it sapped her energy and she barely made it home, throwing off her clothes and climbing into bed, unfortunately conscious enough to pick up the scent of Nick on her sheets.

Damn it all. She *had* to sleep!

But emotion churned inside her—an emotion she'd never felt holding one of her nieces or nephews. This was a new emotion—a heart-rending sorrow that Steffi's mother hadn't really wanted her, while she, Bill, had so longed for the baby she'd conceived, her arms had ached for a year.

And were aching again…

Go to sleep, she ordered herself, and training held true. She fell asleep but dreamt of empty cots and abandoned babies and Nick with his daughter in his arms.

She woke, barely refreshed, at six, and knew she'd better get upstairs so Nick could go to work. Showering, she told herself that if anyone in the world deserved to have his own family it was Nick, and she should be glad for him—*was* glad for him!

Kind of.

'How do mothers know to do all this?' he demanded as she walked into his apartment. 'The notes say she has dinner at five-thirty, a little meat cut up fine with mashed vegetables. It doesn't say what kind of meat or how you can cook a piece of steak while holding a crying baby in your arms and not burn the child, and is she crying because she's hungry or she needs her mother or what? How do I know?'

'You don't,' Bill told him, taking Steffi in her arms and rocking her back and forth until the crying stopped. 'You have to guess, but didn't she have a nap?'

'Of course she had a nap. Bottle and a nap at three, the notes said, and we did that, although I had to put the bottle in the freezer to cool the boiled water before I could give it to her. I can see I'll have to boil water ahead.'

'So you read the notes?' Bill persisted, watching as Nick turned a very large piece of steak on a griddle pan.

'Of course!'

He was cranky and she had to hide a smile so she didn't make things worse.

'The bit that said when she had dinner and what she ate?'

'Of course!' Really cranky now.

'And it didn't occur to you to get it ready while she slept?'

He looked up from the steak, frowning, growling.

'I was busy on the computer.'

'Oh, yes?'

'Well, I obviously can't put a baby seat in my car, can I, so I had to do some research on the safest vehicles for kids to travel in. You've no idea.'

Bill grinned at him, reminded him to turn the steak, then went to the cupboard where one of her sisters-in-law had stacked bottles of additive- and colouring-free baby food. She set Steffi in the highchair, strapped her in, gave her a small plastic spoon to play with, and opened the jar.

'Here,' she said to Nick when she'd warmed the jar in some hot water. 'Feed her this. It won't hurt not to have fresh cooked every now and then, and later, when it's cooled, she can gnaw on a bit of that steak.'

Knowing she would definitely laugh if she watched him feed an infant for the first time, she left him to it, going into the bathroom to run a bath, which Steffi would certainly need.

She'd just set a small plastic duck floating in the water when Nick appeared, both he and Steffi liberally smeared with food.

'I'll get the hang of this!' he muttered as he handed her over, and he was halfway out the door before he added, 'I have to shower. Did I thank you?'

He came back in, embraced them both, then to Bill's astonishment he kissed her, not on the cheek or forehead or even the top of her head, as he was wont to do, but on the lips—*full* on the lips!

'Beyond the call of duty, this, friend Bill,' he said, his voice husky with what couldn't possibly be tears.

Except he hadn't had much sleep, and he'd certainly had the most emotional day of his life, so perhaps...

CHAPTER FIVE

HE'D KISSED BILL on the lips—Bill, his friend, on the lips!

Nick stood under the shower, wondering why this one small incident from an unbelievably momentous day should be occupying his attention to the exclusion of all else.

Including the fact he had a daughter...

Because Bill's lips had felt so soft?

Tasted so sweet?

Or because when he'd tasted that sweetness, felt the softness, he'd also felt a stirring somewhere else?

No, it was because he was shocked and tired—not to mention emotionally exhausted—that kissing Bill had suddenly taken over his mind.

Or he was thinking of it to stop himself worrying over what would become of him and Steffi.

So why was a voice in the back of his head suggesting he kiss Bill again? Perhaps when he left for work, although what the voice was really suggesting was a proper kiss—an in-the-arms kiss, Bill's slim body pressed to his, her lips parting to his invading tongue—

'Out now!'

He spoke the order aloud, hoping to rein in his rampaging thoughts. Far better to think of Steffi and all the problems her arrival was going to cause in his life.

'She'll need some new clothes—just lightweight cotton tops and pants to suit this climate,' Bill said when he walked into the room she'd prepared for Steffi. The little girl was dressed in a long-sleeved pink and white striped suit that covered her from ankles to neck. 'Most of her clothes will be too heavy up here. We'll shop tomorrow, she and I.'

Bill handed him the baby and wandered off, muttering something about getting the bottle ready.

He wanted to follow her, to have a good look at her, although he knew *her* reaction to the kiss wouldn't be written on her face.

In fact, she probably hadn't reacted at all, thinking, if anything, that he'd just happened to miss her cheek.

Deciding to follow her to the kitchen anyway— maybe looking at her would sort out why he'd kissed her lips—he wandered out of the bedroom and stood in the hall, looking into the kitchen where Bill was shaking a bottle to mix the formula.

Her back was to him so he was able to study her— slim legs encased in black leggings, a loose white T-shirt hanging to her thighs, tangled red hair falling below her shoulders, the front bit of it bunched up on the top of her head.

Bill, as he'd seen her thousands of times—so how could he possibly have become attracted to her now?

And why?

Because he hadn't had a regular lover lately?

Lover?

How could he possibly even think that word about Bill?

Was it that insidious longing for a family that had started when Serena had first been pregnant that was making him look at Bill differently?

No, far too convenient an excuse.

Steffi made a gurgling noise and Bill turned, apparently startled to see him there as faint colour spread across her cheeks.

'Have you got time to give Steffi the bottle?' she asked, handing it to him, then, without waiting for a reply, adding, 'I'll get a bib.'

Bill fled, heading for Steffi's room, unable to believe Nick had caught her as she'd been staring vacantly out the kitchen window, thinking about a kiss.

Not just any kiss, but his, Nick's, kiss!

A lip-kiss of all things. Of course, he'd probably aimed for her cheek and she'd moved her head at just the wrong moment.

And although she knew full well he'd have only seen her back view when he'd come into the kitchen, she'd actually blushed—her cheeks burning—at being caught out.

But the kiss had affected her so strangely she hadn't been able to *not* think about it.

Which was crazy as his lips had barely brushed hers, yet she'd felt fire travel from that touch, right through her body, heating her flesh and sending her nerves into a quiver of excitement.

Tiredness, she told herself, and grabbed a bib from where she'd put them in a drawer, intending to hurry back to Nick despite legs heavy with reluctance.

This is totally insane—that was the next bit of information she offered her disordered brain and twitchy body. This is Nick we're talking about.

Nick!

'Bib!'

She handed it to him as he sat on the couch, showing the bottle to Steffi while he tried to work out how best to hold her.

'Like this,' she said, settling the infant in his arms and fixing the bib herself.

Now walk away.

She knew this last bit of advice offered by her few still-functioning brain cells was extremely sensible—even compelling—but how could she walk away from the sight in front of her? Steffi totally absorbed in sucking down her milk, but one hand clutching Nick's little finger and her eyes never moving from his face.

As for Nick, he simply sat, looking down at his daughter, the love he felt for her already written so clearly on his face it hurt Bill's heart to see it.

Rationally she knew that finding he had a daughter was the best thing that had ever happened to Nick, but what lay ahead? Could Steffi be the start of the family he wanted or would he grow to love her more and more then have her snatched away?

Knowing the pain of that kind of loss, Bill could only feel for him—worry for him—yet that was better, surely, than worrying about kisses?

No, one kiss, singular.

One kiss didn't count…

Nick arrived home after a distracted night on duty to a silent home. Tiptoeing, he made his way to Steffi's room but the cot was empty. He assumed Bill was sleeping in the next bedroom, although they hadn't discussed any arrangements—anything at all, really.

The door was open and tucked under a sheet was Bill, making little snuffling noises as she slept, and nestled in beside her was his daughter, also asleep, although an empty bottle on the bedside table suggested that at some time during the night she'd woken up hungry and had needed to be fed again.

Nick stood in the doorway and looked at the pair of them, and felt again an overwhelming surge of love.

For Steffi, of course...

He walked away quietly, into the kitchen, but he'd barely reached the door when he heard a gurgle of laughter. His daughter was awake.

Thinking he'd pick her up and let Bill sleep, he hurried back to the room, but the gurgle had woken Bill as well, and she was smiling tiredly as Steffi played peek-a-boo in the wild red hair.

'Bad night?' Nick asked, moving into the room to scoop Steffi into his arms.

'Not really,' Bill said, sitting up so he couldn't help but notice the minimal nightdress she was wearing, a fine cotton shift that barely covered her small but shapely breasts and clearly showed her body curving down to a tiny waist. 'She woke at three and didn't settle so in the end I gave her another bottle and brought her in with me. So much change and strangeness for the wee mite, I thought she probably needed cuddling, lots of cuddling.'

She grinned and added, 'Then, of course, I was so worried about rolling over and squashing her that I took ages to fall asleep myself. She'll need changing and you'll find clean clothes in the second drawer down in the dresser. I'll be out when I've woken up properly.'

'And put some clothes on,' he muttered to himself as he walked away.

Steffi looked up enquiringly at him and he gave her a reassuring smile, then his nose told him that she really did need changing and that fatherhood wasn't going to be all smiles and gurgling laughter.

Bill was in the kitchen when he'd undressed, cleaned and dressed his daughter again.

'Have you any idea how much excrement a child this size can produce?' he demanded, handing Steffi to Bill so he could have a proper wash himself.

'It's what they're good at, at this age,' Bill told him, as she settled Steffi in the high chair and started asking what she'd like for breakfast.

'Cereal and fruit?' Bill suggested.

Steffi banged her spoon on the tray and Bill grinned at her.

'I thought so,' she said, pulling the box of baby cereal and a small jar of puréed fruit from the cupboard. 'Now your dad's clean, he can feed you.'

'Oh, no!' Nick retorted. 'I did it last night. I'll make our breakfast—coffee and toast do you? I haven't shopped but Bob made sure there were some essentials here.'

Bill agreed that coffee and toast would be fine. She lifted the highchair close to the breakfast bar and perched on a stool so she could feed Steffi while they had breakfast.

Nick tried to focus on what he was doing, but making coffee and toast demanded little in the way of concentration so the domesticity of the situation attracted most of his attention. He watched Bill, noticed the way her lips parted slightly as she spooned food into Steffi's mouth, saw the concentration on Bill's face, but something else...

Concern?

Something more he couldn't understand?

'I know Serena said she was used to being cared for by strangers, but you'd think she must be missing if not her mother at least her grandmother.'

Bill's statement cut into his thoughts.

Had she been worrying about Steffi's well-being while he tried to guess at something deeper?

'You'd think so,' he agreed. 'So, what can we do?'

Bill frowned at him but he knew the frown was for her thoughts, not for him—at least, he hoped so.

'I think all we can do is give her lots and lots of physical love—cuddles, talking, kisses, songs—using her name and telling her we love her. I've no idea how much infants understand at different ages, but I don't know what else we can do.'

Nick felt his chest squeeze. Hadn't love always been Bill's answer to everything? Love for her friends, her pets, her family. The arguments they'd had over love—he claiming it was something poets and musicians made up to write about, she firm in her belief it made the world go round.

But now he'd felt this thing called love—for what else could the emotion he felt towards his daughter be?—he realised that while it might not make the world go round, it was probably all they could do to help Steffi feel secure—give her lots and lots of love.

Show her love with talk and cuddles.

But was it wrong of him to expect Bill to be doing this when Steffi wasn't Bill's child?

Was it something to do with *her* relationship to Steffi that was causing the shadows he kept catching on Bill's face?

'Write a list of what you need at the supermarket and Steffi and I will go there after we've bought her some tropical clothes,' the woman he was worrying about said as she scraped the last of the cereal out of the bowl and spooned it into Steffi's mouth, neatly wiping off the excess with a small facecloth she'd had the foresight to have nearby.

He'd show her love and he'd learn to do all these things, Nick told himself, and concentrating on learning all he could about caring for his daughter would distract him from the wayward thoughts he was having about Bill.

'I could shop later when I've had a sleep,' he said, knowing he needed to start right now because his wayward thoughts were increasing despite the fact he and Bill must have breakfasted together like this—yes, a thousand times...

Except he hadn't felt his gut clench when she smiled at him—not once in those thousand times.

'I think for a few days at least your spare time should be spent with Steffi, so you learn the rhythms of her life and you get to know each other better. Write a list and we'll shop while you sleep, then this afternoon she'll be all yours.'

It made sense so he wrote a list—a good distraction—although if Bill was staying here he needed to consult her on what she liked to eat.

'Same as you, remember, steak and salad, lamb cutlets and salad, roast lamb—basic food. Put what you want in the way of snacks and drinks on the list, I'll do the rest. If I'm to be lolling around here for the week I might as well do the evening meal. We can gradually shift Steffi's evening meal a little later, and with you working nights you need to eat early so we can all eat together, which, the sensible Kirsten tells me, is a good habit to get into.'

Except it makes us seem like a family—the thing I wanted—but we're not, Nick thought as he left the room to find a pen and notepad, really leaving the room because the distraction of Bill's long, tanned legs tucked up on the stool was stronger than the distraction of learning to look after his daughter.

One week, that's all it would be, Bill promised herself as Nick left the room. Within a week she'd have settled Steffi into her new, if temporary home, found a decent, reliable nanny to give Nick back-up care when he was working and she could leave him to get to know his daughter on his own.

The 'if temporary' part worried her. It was all very well for Serena to tell Nick they'd 'talk' when she returned, but knowing Nick there was no way, now he knew about her, that he would give up his daughter.

No way he could, Bill suspected, remembering the besotted look on Nick's face.

She sighed and reminded herself that she needed to be careful too. Even more careful than Nick, for Steffi wasn't and never would be her daughter, so falling in love with the wee mite was just not on.

Detached—that's how she had to be. She could love Steffi as she loved her nieces and nephews, but stay detached…

She'd sent Nick off to have a sleep and was clearing

up the kitchen when he reappeared, clad only in long-ish boxer shorts that he must wear as pyjamas. Her eyes were drawn inexorably towards his chest and were so focussed there she hadn't a clue what he was saying.

'I missed that,' she said, cursing inwardly because her voice came out all breathy.

'I was saying you can't take Steffi to the shops—no car seat.'

Desperate to distract herself from that chest, Bill lifted Steffi out of the highchair and set her on the floor, handing her a couple of wooden spoons and a sauce-pan to bang.

'I've got a car seat,' she responded, 'and whichever sister-in-law brought it insisted on installing it so she knew it was secure. She even adjusted the straps to fit Steffi. And there's a stroller in the car as well, so we're all set,' she said, skipping out of Steffi's reach as the toddler decided hitting legs was more fun than hitting a saucepan.

'You've thought of everything,' Nick grumbled as he turned back towards his bedroom, although he did relent, swinging back to smile and say, 'I have thanked you, haven't I?'

To Bill's dismay she felt a blush rising up her neck towards her cheeks as she remembered just how he'd thanked her. Thinking quickly, she bent down to lift Steffi in her arms to shield her so-transparent reaction from Nick.

'Of course you have,' she mumbled against Steffi's fluff of hair.

Now he'd never sleep because *now* he was remembering the kiss. Nick headed for his bedroom, muttering under his breath. Bad enough he'd had to fight the impulse to touch Bill—on the shoulder, knee, neck, cheek—all through breakfast, but by reminding him that he *had* thanked her, she'd reminded him of the kiss.

He couldn't do it—couldn't have her living here while this peculiar reaction to her was going on in his body.

Not that he could manage without her.

Although…?

Running through his roster in his head, he remembered he had three days off coming up soon.

When?

Five nights on then three off, wasn't that the system here at Willowby?

So two more nights on duty, and by the end of his three days off, the hospital human resources department should have found a locum to fill in for him. Two weeks, that's all he'd asked for.

He'd need to sleep for some time on the first of his days off, but he could sleep when Steffi slept. He'd show Bill over the next two afternoons how well he could manage his daughter so his friend wouldn't be worried when he told her he could cope without her.

And on that cheery note he fell asleep, only to dream of a long-legged, red-haired siren running through his life, always just ahead of him, taunting and tantalising him but never within reach.

Something really good was cooking when he woke up, and the aroma permeating the house was more than enough to tempt him out of bed.

'What *are* you cooking?' he demanded as he came into the kitchen, starving because he'd slept through lunch.

'Casserole for dinner,' Bill replied, 'but there's ham in the fridge if you want to make a sandwich for a late lunch. I'm doing a big casserole of meat and veggies in the slow cooker so you can freeze it in meal-sized portions and always have something you can shove in the microwave when it's been a bad day.'

Nick was pulling butter and ham from the refrigerator as she finished talking and from where he was the words had an ominous sound.

'What kind of bad day?'

Bill turned from where she was adjusting knobs on the steriliser and smiled at him.

It had to be hunger that was making his heart miss a beat while a desire stronger than he'd ever felt before surged through his body.

Sure the state of his arousal would be obvious, he dumped the makings of his lunch on the table, mumbled, 'Tell me later—I should shower before I eat,' and fled the kitchen.

It had to be the dream, he decided as he stood under the shower that was not quite cold but definitely cool.

And if it wasn't the dream—if he was going to get an erection of mammoth proportions every time Bill smiled at him—then one of them had to go.

Now.

A not unhappy wail from Steffi's bedroom made him amend that to *soon*.

Very soon.

He dried himself, pulled on clothes then, thinking Bill would still be busy in the kitchen, went to retrieve his daughter from her cot.

She'd pulled herself up and was peering at him over the top, smilingly delighted with her achievement.

'Yes, you are a clever girl,' he assured her, lifting her and holding her close, feeling again the somersault of love this small mortal had brought into his life.

And because, for at least the next few days, they both needed Bill, she would have to stay.

'So I'll have to keep my mind on you and the problems you're causing in my life, young lady,' he told Steffi as he put her on the change table and began the process of nappy-changing.

'Yuck!' he said, as he undid her nappy.

The word brought a crow of delight from his daughter, but as he cleaned up the little bottom he noticed redness.

Nappy rash.

He knew the words, but treatment?

With one hand on Steffi's tummy he surveyed the array of tubes and jars of cream on hand beside the change table.

'This thick stuff?' he wondered, waving the jar in front of the little girl.

Steffi gurgled her approval, but it was the 'Well done!' from the doorway that confirmed he'd chosen the correct remedy.

'I need to read the notes again,' he said as he smeared the white cream liberally all over Steffi's little bottom, but only part of his mind was on the job, the rest of it thinking about Bill—wondering why on earth, after all these years, he should suddenly be attracted to her.

He finished changing Steffi and, remembering she usually had a drink of water after her sleep, carried her into the kitchen where Bill had a covered container of boiled water ready for any occasion.

'I'll get the cup,' Bill offered, and she filled the little

cup and screwed the lid on, handing it not to Nick but to Steffi, who grasped one of the handles and tried to manoeuvre the sipping part into her mouth.

'Can't quite manage it, kid?' Bill teased, and she held the cup so Steffi could suck from it.

They were close, so close, Nick holding the baby, Bill with one hand on Steffi's back, helping her to drink, then gold-brown eyes lifted and met his, and a heaviness in Nick's chest stopped his breathing.

It seemed their gazes held for minutes, although seconds seemed more likely, the spell broken when Bill smiled and said, rather breathlessly, 'Well, isn't this the silliest thing ever?'

And without waiting for an answer, she took Steffi from his arms, said, 'Get your lunch,' and disappeared with his daughter into the living room.

He made his sandwich and considered staying right there in the kitchen to eat it, but that would be even sillier than whatever was happening between them. Bill's statement had confirmed she, too, was feeling the attraction, so surely the best way to deal with it would be to talk about it.

Calmly and sensibly discuss it—maybe work out some rational reason why this should be happening between them now.

He took his sandwich into the living room, where Bill was lying on the floor, Steffi bouncing up and down on her stomach.

Nick sank into an armchair, took a bite of his sandwich, a sip of tea, then decided there was no time like the present to get it out into the open.

It?

Could something like the desire he was feeling for this woman be encompassed in a simple 'it'?

'It must be that we haven't seen much of each other over the last few years,' he said, then worried that perhaps she hadn't been talking about attraction earlier and he'd gone and made a fool of himself.

She peered at him around Steffi's head.

'You think?'

'Well, something's happened, hasn't it?' he grumbled. 'Come on, it's not like you not to be offering an opinion—several opinions, in fact.'

'About what?' she asked, all innocence, shifting so Steffi was now on the floor but remaining close to her so Steffi could play with her hair.

'You know damn well what.'

He was growling now, certain the woman was taunting him, stretched out so languidly on his floor, legs, hips, waist, breasts offered up to him, while the lips that had tasted so soft and sweet quivered with a little smile that was driving him to distraction.

He finished his sandwich, refusing to play her game, but when Steffi's attention was fully absorbed with a toy that made the most extraordinary noises when she pushed buttons and pulled on levers, Bill sat up, moving closer to him but stopping just short of resting her head on his knees, as she'd done countless times in the past when they had been no more than friends.

Which they were now, weren't they?

'Remember us sitting like this while we sorted out one or other of our love lives?' she asked, following his thoughts with such precision it was scary.

'Or sorting out the problems of the world,' he reminded her.

She nodded, then put her hand on his knee.

It was nothing more than a friendly gesture, yet his skin beneath that hand burned as if she'd branded him. He wanted to lift it off so the pain would go away, and he wanted it to stay there—for ever...

Silence fell between them, although the bells and whistles continued to rattle around the room from Steffi's toy, and her giggles of delight distracted Nick so when Bill spoke he didn't catch what she was saying until she was well into her statement.

'—because your life is complicated enough as it is right now, what with Steffi, and Serena coming back to talk. We don't need to make it more complicated by having an affair.'

'Who mentioned an affair?' he demanded.

She grinned at him.

'Are you saying that isn't what your body wants?'

'Of course it is—no, of course it isn't. Why an affair anyway?'

'Well, I hardly think it could turn into a for-ever-and-ever thing, could it?'

She ran her finger over his lips, freezing his thoughts, although he'd have liked to ask why it couldn't be for ever and ever...

'Nick, the attraction is there,' she continued gently. 'It's inconvenient, nothing more than that. I'm saying I think we have to live with the inconvenience of it. We'll both be busy enough with work and caring for Steffi, and once you're sorted with a nanny I won't need to be living here so it will be easier. But your world has been turned upside down—mine too, to a lesser extent—so it's only natural that our bodies should be turning to each other for support.'

'It's not support my body wants from yours,' Nick growled, taking that tantalising finger and sucking gently on it.

'Or mine from yours, to tell the truth,' Bill admitted, shivering a little as she removed her finger and leaned against his legs, resting her head on his knees, licking at his skin to get a taste of Nick—the kind of taste she'd never considered she could ever want.

'And you can stop that,' he told her, easing her away from his legs and settling on the floor to play with Steffi. 'Go and do whatever you have to do—we'll be right until dinner and bathtime. See you around five?'

So, that was it for the attraction conversation, Bill realised. She hauled herself off the floor, bent to kiss the top of Steffi's head as she said goodbye, and left the apartment.

But she couldn't shut the door on thoughts of Nick.

Nick as a man.

Nick as a desirable, sexy man who was stirring her body into an agony of wanting.

She pulled her mobile out of her pocket and phoned him.

'I suppose the alternative would be for us to have a quick, passionate fling and get it out of our systems then we could go back to where we were,' she said as soon as he answered.

'And just when could we conduct this fling?' he demanded. 'I can't even answer the phone without my daughter trying to wrestle it from me, and we'd no sooner get to the interesting part than she'd be yelling from her cot. *Coitus interruptus* at its best.'

'At least I wouldn't get pregnant,' Bill told him,

chuckling at the image he'd described. 'But you're right, best we just ignore the whole thing and hope it will go away.'

'Like a really, really bad cold,' Nick grumped, then he disconnected the call.

CHAPTER SIX

BILL DID BUSY stuff to distract herself, washing, vacu-
uming, putting fresh sheets on the bed, and clearing
debris from the refrigerator as she'd be eating at Nick's
for this week at least.

Food, refrigerator, Nick's—

She grabbed her phone again and hit Nick's speed-
dial number.

'Not another suggestion about our sex lives?' he muttered as he answered.

'Of course not,' Bill told him. 'Something far more
important than sex. I don't know why I didn't think of
it earlier but, Nick, we haven't told Gran about Steffi,
and if we don't someone else is sure to now all the de
Grootes know, but what do we say?'

She heard Nick groan.

'Damn and blast—I should have gone over yesterday
but yesterday was a disaster from start to finish. Can
I borrow your car? I'll take her now. We'll have time
before dinner—but then there's her nap.'

'She'll sleep in the car and, yes, we'll go in my car.
I'll drive.'

'You'll come?'

Nick sounded so surprised Bill had to laugh.

'Didn't we always face Gran, or my parents for that matter, together when we were in trouble?'

'I'm not sure trouble quite covers this situation,' Nick replied, sounding so uneasy Bill felt a pang of sympathy for him.

Better that than lust, she realised as she told him to pull himself together, grab a brightly coloured bag off the chest of drawers—'It's got spare nappies, cream, clothes and baby wipes in it'—and meet her in the car park.

She brought her car close to the lift and had the back door open when Nick and Steffi emerged. Taking Steffi from him, she strapped her in, aware Nick was watching every move, learning all the time.

Aware too of Nick as a man—the impossible dream...

'I wondered when I was going to meet my great-granddaughter. Whillimina's family have been phoning all day,' Gran greeted them, then she lifted Steffi into her arms and smiled down at her. 'And don't bother telling me what it's all about,' she said, addressing both Nick and Bill. 'I'm too old to be bothered with details. I just need to know the little girl is being properly looked after, and that I get to see her at least once a week and mind her from time to time.'

'Oh, Gran,' Nick said, his voice so husky the words barely came out, then he hugged the woman who'd brought him up, his arms easily encompassing both her and his daughter. 'I'm sorry I didn't let you know about her earlier but it's all come as such a shock.'

Gran led them into the living room and waved for them to sit down. Steffi was playing with the glass beads around Gran's neck, apparently quite comfort-able on the older woman's knee.

'I'm glad you're back, of course,' Gran said, 'but when you made the arrangements to return you didn't know about young Steffi here. Things will change, you know.'

'And how,' Nick told her, but Gran wasn't finished.

'Not just in adjusting to having a child, but now you know about Steffi you will have different priorities and I don't want you to feel you have to honour your contract in Willowby because of me. You were a good boy and you've grown into a fine man, and you keep in touch with me more than most young men would with their parents or grandparents, but you have to live your own life, remember.'

What was she saying?

Nick ran her words through his head, thinking he could ask Bill later what she'd thought of them, but Bill had excused herself to make some tea.

'Once I've sorted out the care arrangements, Steffi won't make too much difference in my life,' he told Gran, who smiled and raised her eyebrows.

'We'll see,' she said gently. 'We'll see.'

Bored with the beads, Steffi was trying to climb off Gran's knee so Nick rescued her and put her on the floor, pulling a stacking toy out of the bag Bill had ob-viously prepared for outings such as this.

'And Whillimina?' Gran asked, nodding her head towards the kitchen. 'I hear she's helping you take care of Steffi.'

'Only until the hospital can give me some time off and we get a nanny to look after her when I go back to work.'

It sounded like an excuse and he knew Gran would pick up on it.

'Is it fair on her, considering all that happened to her in the past?' Gran asked, right on cue.

All that's happened in the past?

Nick wanted to ask Gran what she meant, but Bill came through the door at that moment, carrying a tray with teapot, milk and sugar, cups and saucers and a plate of biscuits on it.

'Set it down on the sideboard where Steffi won't be able to reach it,' Gran said, removing a Dresden figurine from her great-granddaughter's hands.

Bill poured the tea and the rest of the visit was taken up with local gossip and general conversation.

'Do you think someone's told her about Serena and what happened that she was so incurious about how a baby lobbed into my life?' Nick asked Bill as they drove back towards the apartment.

Bill considered the matter for a while then shook her head.

'I doubt it. I didn't tell my lot much—just that you had a small child and needed stuff for her. Some of my sisters-in-law are probably dying to know, but most people would just shrug and accept it. I think with Gran she knows you'll talk about it when you're ready and she's willing to wait until then.'

'Talk about it when I'm ready?'

Nick's voice was so loud Steffi gave a little whimper then settled back into sleep.

'How can I ever be ready when I haven't a clue what's really going on?' Nick asked in a more subdued but still panicked tone. 'So I know about Steffi and she's here with me now, but what of the future? What will Serena's "talk" entail? I want to stay here, Bill, to work here, for at least for a year and probably longer. I'd actually been thinking for ever...'

His voice tailed off and he was silent for a moment, before he asked, 'Can we drive to the beach? Not Wood-choppers but Sunrise, where we can sit in the car and look out at the water.'

Bill understood exactly what he was asking—understood why as well. As teenagers they'd often sat on the headland at Sunrise Beach, looking out at the sea while they'd solved the problems of the world.

Or their love lives...

Bill parked the car in a corner of the car park and they sat in silence, Steffi asleep in her car seat.

'I came here to see Gran and be with her,' Nick finally said, 'but, in truth, the life I'd decided to lead was palling. You can have too much fun, you know.'

He sounded so serious Bill had to fight an urge to laugh, but instead turned towards him and took his hand.

'It was the family thing, I imagine,' she told him. 'Once you'd had that thought—seen the image of yourself as a family man in your head—it would have been hard to shift, and Willowby would have been a natural place for you to settle.'

He lifted her hand and dropped a light kiss on her fingers.

'I guess so, although at the time I didn't dwell on the family thing for long. Serena had squashed the idea so quickly and completely I thought I'd put it out of my head until quite recently when coming up here mainly for Gran made me think of it again.'

'You could never have put it out of your heart,' Bill

murmured. 'Not having had a real family of your own. Once the idea sneaked in it would have been hard to dislodge.'

He squeezed her fingers.

'I suppose you're right, but what next, Bill? What do I do? What do we do?'

Bill retrieved her hand before he could excite it—and her—further, though a light kiss and a hand squeeze was hardly erotic foreplay.

'*We* do nothing,' she said, 'not as a "we". But you look after Steffi with me or a nanny to help and you go to work and visit Gran and do all the things you intended doing when you came up here.'

'Except,' she added, remembering the leggy blondes at breakfast, 'the rushing out to the islands to have a wild old time on your days off. Later, when Steffi gets to know you and feels at home, you can have a social life again, though judging from my family's experiences late nights are severely limited by their children's habit of getting up at an unreasonably early hour in the morning.'

Thinking she'd handled the conversation quite well, for all the churning in her stomach as she'd denied the 'we', Bill sat back in her seat and looked out towards the islands, noticing how calm and clear the water was, thinking a swim might clear her head.

'So, that's me done,' Nick said. 'What about you?'

She turned towards him.

'Me?'

His eyes were shadowed, his mouth serious, and she wondered what on earth could be coming next.

'Gran asked if it was fair to you to have you minding Steffi. To quote Gran, "considering all that happened".'

He touched Bill's cheek and she felt the shiver of re-action—or possibly despair—rattle through her body.

'What happened? Is this to do with Nigel? With you calling off the wedding?'

His voice was deep with understanding, with sym-pathy—with love, the friendship-love they'd shared for ever—and Bill felt something crack inside her.

The lump in her throat was too big to swallow so she made do with a nod.

'Tell me.'

It wasn't an order, more a whispered plea, but sud-denly the lump disappeared and she found she could talk about that time, about discovering she was preg-nant a month before the wedding, Nigel's horrified re-action—'people will think that's why we married, we can't have that'. His demand she have an abortion, her realisation that he was a shallow, selfish, social-climb-ing toadie and calling off the wedding. Then—

'But what happened?' Nick asked, obviously enough as she certainly didn't have a baby now.

'I miscarried,' she said, and felt his arms close around her, drawing her to his chest, holding her tightly as he told her how sorry he was, how stupid she was not to have told him, how he'd have come to her, she should have known that.

When the hug turned from sympathy to something else she afterwards wasn't sure, but somehow they shifted their positions and Nick was kissing her full on the lips.

The sun was shining, the sea was calm, Steffi was asleep...

Bill kissed him back.

The world didn't come to an end.

Anything but!

In fact, as Bill responded, meeting the demands of Nick's lips with demands of her own, her body came to life in a way she'd never felt before. Heat surged through her, her blood on fire, while her breasts grew heavy with desire and the ache between her thighs made her twist in her seat as she tried to ease the longing.

'This is stupid.' she managed to mutter as Nick's hand left her cheek and roved across the skin on her neck, sliding down to cup one heavy breast. 'Idiocy!'

'I know,' he mumbled back, nuzzling now at the base of her neck and causing goose-bumps all down her spine.

But the kissing didn't stop, the desperation in it suggestive of a starving man needing to eat his fill in case the meal should be his last.

Bill's head tried to rationalise the situation—this was Nick, he was in trouble at the moment, shocked by the discovery he had a daughter, he needed comforting.

And she'd just told him what had happened—she was entitled to a little comfort herself.

But as the intensity of her response to Nick's kisses grew, she lost track of the excuses and gave herself up to the pleasure of kissing Nick and being kissed by him.

It wasn't Steffi waking up that stopped them but the arrival of another vehicle, a battered four-wheel drive, pulling up not at the other side of the car park, in spite of it being empty, but right beside them.

They broke apart, and seeing Nick's flushed face Bill knew she'd be fiery red herself. To hide her telltale cheeks, she turned in her seat, pretending she was checking Steffi, who still slept on, blithely unaware of the behaviour of her father and his best friend.

'And what are you doing here, Whillimina Florence? Not necking with some worthless boy, surely?'

Dirk, the youngest of her six brothers, a mad keen fisherman no doubt heading for the rocks below where they were parked.

'We're actually enjoying a few moments' peace and quiet while Steffi sleeps,' Nick responded, getting out of the car and coming around the hood to shake Dirk's hand—shielding Bill from him at the same time.

'Or we were until you arrived,' Nick added.

'Heard about the kid,' Dirk said, grinning at Nick and peering into the back of the vehicle to check his information was correct. 'Bet that's put a dampener on your social life.'

'Maybe it needed one,' Nick replied, and Bill knew he meant it, though she wondered, apart from his sudden longing for a family, if something more had happened to her friend.

Perhaps he'd really loved Serena and had been hurt by her refusal to marry him?

Oh, damn and blast. Surely not?

Although it would explain the passion of his kiss.

Rejected by the woman he adored, he'd taken off for overseas and now, back in Australia, had turned to the next one that came along, who just happened to be her, Bill…

She wanted to wail in protest and bang her head against the steering-wheel, then bang Nick's head against anything handy.

How stupid could one woman be? Kissing him back when she knew nothing could happen between them—knew, whatever had happened in the past between him and Serena, Serena would be back…

'Sorry, but I have to feed the kid then get to work,' Nick was saying to Dirk, 'but if I can organise Gran to sit with her for a few hours later in the week, I'd love to join you on the rocks. I'll give you a call.'

Organise Gran to sit with Steffi?

So Nick, too, had realised just how stupid the kiss had been, and he was already working out how to get *her* out of his life—well, possibly not right out but he was definitely figuring how to put distance between the two of them.

'Fishing with Dirk?' Bill asked when she'd said goodbye to her brother and Nick was back in the car.

He turned and smiled.

'Simple pleasures,' he said. That fitted with all the other stuff he'd said, but it also wiped away any memory of the kiss—drew a line under it without it being mentioned while telling her in no uncertain terms that there *was* a line, and it would not be crossed again.

Driving back to the apartment block, she wasn't sure whether to be glad or sorry. Common sense, of which she'd once had plenty, told her she was glad. She could count it as an aberration and tuck it away deep in her memory and with any luck forget it altogether.

That's likely, an errant voice in her head piped up, but she knew she had to ignore it.

Somehow he had to ease himself out of this situation without hurting Bill, Nick decided as she drove him towards the apartments. The hurt she'd already endured—hurt he'd known nothing about—was more than enough and Gran was right—how fair was it to expect Bill to take care of his child now he knew what she'd suffered?

As for that Nigel…

No, Nick told himself as he felt anger against the man building in his gut, forget the past and work out how to get through the next little while.

He had to get over the attraction business and definitely avoid physical contact because kissing her had made the situation worse. He had to forget the hunger he'd tasted on her lips, a hunger that had met and matched his own.

His future was too uncertain.

Well, not uncertain in one way. Steffi was his future and if he could just concentrate on that and ease Bill out of his life—or at least out of his apartment—as quickly as possible, then everything should be okay.

He glanced at her, and saw the little frown puckering the clear skin of her forehead and wanted more than anything to touch her, to assure her everything would be all right, but the kiss had made it impossible for him to touch her—possibly ever again. The kiss had shifted their relationship into a place where it couldn't be...

'If you cook a potato and mash it with some peas and a little gravy and carrot from the casserole in the slow cooker, I think Steffi will eat that for her dinner.'

Nick's turn to frown.

Was that all Bill had been frowning about?

Steffi's dinner?

Could she have shoved her emotional confession back into some box in her mind and switched back to practical Bill?

Could she have dismissed the *kiss* so easily?

They'd reached the entrance to the car park and she was leaning out to press the code that opened the big doors so he couldn't see her face, but even if he could see it, would he be able to read it?

The Bill he'd kissed, and who'd kissed him back with mind-blowing enthusiasm, was a Bill he didn't know at all.

'I'll drop you both off and be back in time for you to go to work,' she added as she pulled up next to the lift. 'I need to pop over and see Kirsten to ask her about nannies—she had one when she went back to work after her kids started school—just part time, some kind of share arrangement with another mother. I know there are a couple of agencies in town but she'll know which one is best.'

Nick took in the information, aware as he did so that Bill was intent on distancing herself from him, just as he'd intended doing from her. Yet somehow it aggravated him that she'd moved first.

Pathetic.

That's what he was.

'Well, go on, out you get, and don't forget your daughter,' Bill told him, back to her old bossy self, which aggravated Nick even more.

But he got out, unstrapped Steffi from her car seat—a feat in itself—and carried her and the colourful bag into the elevator, refusing to wave as Bill took off, tyres squealing on the concrete floor.

CHAPTER SEVEN

'HA! YOU WEAKENED,' Nick said to Bill when she turned up an hour before he was due to go to work. 'Bet you thought I couldn't do the bath myself.'

This, he'd decided as he'd fed and bathed his daughter, was how he was going to play things. As if nothing had ever happened between them.

The tightening of his body suggested it hadn't totally accepted this idea but he soldiered on.

'Nothing to it,' he said, pointing to where a pyjama-clad Steffi was playing with toys on the living-room floor.

'Until you need to shower yourself,' Bill said, smiling as Steffi noticed her and began to crawl towards her, gurgling a welcome.

'I did wonder about that and decided that's why you had the playpen thing. Pop her in there with some toys and shower quickly.'

'Well done, you,' Bill said, swinging Steffi up into her arms so Nick wasn't sure if her praise was for him or his daughter. 'But now I'm here I'll read her a story while you do whatever you have to do to get ready for work, okay?'

Bill turned back to face him as she added the last word, and he knew she was asking something else.

Like were things okay between them?

Or, dread thought, was it okay if they never mentioned the kiss?

'The casserole was fantastic,' he said by way of reply, 'but Bob didn't include containers for freezing things when he furnished this place so I've left it all in the pot.'

He decided that had answered the first possible question—a normal Nick-Bill conversation. The second question was unanswerable.

He showered, shaved and dressed for work, returning to the living room to find Steffi already asleep in Bill's arms.

'You want to pop her into bed?' Bill asked, and he bent and lifted his daughter, smelling the baby smell of her and feeling his heart swell again with love and pride.

Knowing that, whatever happened in the future, Steffi's welfare would come first.

He carried her into the bedroom and laid her down gently in her cot. Bill had followed him, carrying a small ornamental angel. She fiddled with it for a moment, plugging a lead from it into a power point then pressing one of the angel's wings.

'Intercom,' she explained. 'I put the receiver near my bed so I can hear her if she wakes in the night. Kirsten gave it to me this afternoon, along with some info about nannies. We can talk about that tomorrow.'

And with that she slipped away, leaving him watching his sleeping daughter, trying to take in the enormous changes that had happened in his life in three short days.

'Not that I regret them,' he told the sleeping Steffi, reaching down to pull a light sheet over her.

He called goodbye to Bill, who'd disappeared into the bedroom she was using, and left for work, hoping it would be a busy night so he didn't have time to think about Bill or bedrooms or anything other than work really.

Bill heard the door close behind him and came out of the bedroom, telling herself how pathetic she was, hiding away like that. Although she'd had a valid excuse, putting new batteries into the receiver of the intercom and setting it up on the table next to her bed.

In the kitchen she peered into the slow cooker, cursing herself for not slipping back down to her apartment before Nick left, to get some containers to freeze the leftovers.

Tomorrow would do.

Helping herself to a plateful, she sat down to eat it, wondering how long it would take to find a nanny and wondering if *not* living here with Nick would make things better or worse as far as the attraction went.

She'd barely finished her meal when her mobile trilled.

The hospital!

Nick?

Answer the damn thing, she told herself, and did so.

'Mass panic,' Angie, the triage sister, told her. 'I know you've got time off for some reason or other but we need anyone we can get. A backpackers' minibus overturned on the bypass, fourteen passengers and driver all with various injuries. The first admissions will be at the hospital in fifteen minutes. Can you come?'

Thank heaven she'd seen Kirsten just that afternoon was Bill's first thought.

'I'll be there, possibly not within fifteen minutes but as soon as I can get there,' she told Angie, then she phoned Kirsten, who'd offered to babysit any time, explaining, as she'd said it, that her two were off at her mother's place for a few days and being school holidays she was free herself.

She could also ask Kirsten to bring freezer containers...

'Kirsten's minding Steffi,' Bill said, finding Nick as soon as she walked into the ER, knowing if he saw her there before she explained, he'd panic.

He was bent over a stretcher, listening to the ambo explain the treatment that had already been given to the patient, but he nodded to show he'd heard Bill's words then smiled.

'Glad you're here,' he said briefly but with such genuine gratitude that Bill knew the situation was dire.

'Second ambulance two minutes out,' Angie said, when Bill approached the triage desk. 'I've more doctors coming in but no one to take this patient yet. Will you meet and assess? Nick can join you when and if he stabilises the young woman he's with now.'

Bill nodded, and grabbed a trolley, knowing the ambulance would have to turn around to return to the accident. They'd move the patient onto it, quickly transferring her to hospital monitoring equipment so the ambulance equipment would be free.

The patient was another young girl, blunt chest

trauma, intubated and with fluid flowing into her, but Bill could hear a wheezing noise and wondered if the oxygen she was getting was flowing out as quickly as it flowed in.

'Open pneumothorax,' the ambo said after they'd settled her on the trolley. He lifted the sheet that covered the young woman and pointed to a large sterile dressing on the left-hand side of her chest. 'Freak accident. She must have been holding her backpack on her knee when the bus tipped over and a weird silver thing went into her chest. We had to remove it to put the patch on her, but it's there near her legs somewhere in case the docs need to see what it is.'

He handed Bill the paperwork and took the empty stretcher back to his ambulance.

The 'weird silver thing' was of no importance to Bill or the young woman right now. The patch was acting as a flutter valve, one side open to allow air to escape, but the wound would have to be closed, and quickly. Were there surgeons coming in? Another nurse arrived and together they assessed the patient, knowing everything they did, even in an emergency, had to be checked and rechecked.

The young woman's breathing was slow and shallow and oxygen levels in her blood were veering towards dangerously low.

Thoracostomy!

Did every nurse's head have words rarely thought of just sitting there waiting to be thrown up when necessary?

'See if there's a doctor free,' Bill said to her assistant. 'She needs a drainage tube put into her chest to get rid of any fluid collecting in there, then the wound closed as soon as possible. But if we can get the drainage going she'll be more comfortable and hopefully her blood gases will improve.'

The nurse returned, almost inevitably, with Nick, but this was work and in a work situation personal issues were forgotten.

Bill explained while he examined the patient, then, taking care to keep away from the wound, anaesthetised a small area of her chest. Bill had the thoracostomy needle and drainage tube ready for him and within minutes the drain was in, fluid and blood flowing from it.

Lifting the sterile dressing, Nick examined the wound.

'She needs it closed,' he said, and turned to the young nurse. 'Can you find out how soon a surgeon will be here and where this lass is on the triage list? I can close it if no one else is available.'

Of course you could, Bill thought, again realising just how competent an ER doctor Nick was, but it was the realisation of why he was so good—his time with the army—that made her heart ache. That time must also have deepened his desire for a family. Well, now he had one—or part of one. With Serena's return he'd have the real thing, which was why she herself had to butt out right now.

Rob Darwin arrived before she had time to become melancholy over this decision—one, in fact, she'd already made.

'Two surgeons up in OR with the bus driver who looks like losing his leg, but if you're happy to do this, I'll assist,' he said to Nick.

Around them they could hear the noise of other nurses and doctors shouting for this or that, the chaos of a multiple casualty accident continuing, but within the cubicle everyone's concentration was on the patient, on closing the young woman's chest so her heart and lungs could function properly.

Nick worked with such precision, cutting more skin around the wound, cleaning the flap he'd need later to close the hole, clearing blood clots from deep inside, Rob holding back the skin while Bill irrigated the flesh beneath. Whatever had driven in had gone between ribs but had torn the cartilage connecting them.

Carefully Nick put the muscles and tissue back together again, stitching and stapling until finally the wound was sealed by the young woman's own skin, drawn tightly across her ribs.

'What did it?' he asked as he straightened up, leaving Bill to apply the dressing.

'Something silver—it should be by her legs,' Bill told him. 'The ambos think it was in her backpack, which she was holding on her knees.'

Nick felt beneath the sheet and found the small silver statue of a cat with its right paw raised.

'If it's a good luck charm, it didn't work, did it?' he said, returning it to its place beside the girl. 'That paw must have gone straight through her chest when the accident happened. Perhaps she had it in her hand at the time, showing it to someone.'

'Well, she's had some good luck landing in a hospital where an ER doctor can close her chest with a minimum of fuss,' Rob said, then he turned to Bill. 'Can I grab you a coffee?'

As soon as the words were out he must have realised his mistake and offered to get one for Nick as well, but as an approaching siren told them another patient was on the way, they both refused, and Rob went off to refresh himself before heading back into the fray.

'He's still hopeful of getting a date,' Nick said, his voice strained but that could be stress. 'Perhaps if you went out with him you'd find the spark.'

And put a distance between you and me, Bill thought, but didn't say it, knowing it was exactly what Nick was thinking.

'I think that's called using people and I'll deal with the stupid situation between us in my own way,' she snapped, then headed for the entrance to prepare for the next arrival, although as she watched the ambos unload the patient, she wondered if going out with Rob might not be a good idea.

Not all romances began with instant attraction.

And Rob was relatively new in town and lonely, and by going out with him she could introduce him to some other women and maybe he'd find someone who *did* feel a spark.

So, rather than using him, she'd be doing him a good turn and at the same time distancing herself from Nick .

By midnight all the patients had been stabilised, some flown south for further treatment, some hospitalised and the lucky few with minor injuries had been packed off to their hostel. Not wanting to keep Kirsten up later than necessary, Bill signed off and headed home.

'No trouble at all,' Kirsten said. 'She's a gorgeous little thing, isn't she? I've been watching her sleep. What's the story?'

Bill sighed.

'Who knows really? The bits I do know are so unbelievable I don't like to think about them. Briefly, Nick thought his girlfriend was having an abortion but she didn't and now there's Steffi, and right now her mother is in New York, which is why the baby's here with Nick, and after that—who knows?'

'Nick won't let her go,' Kirsten said, 'Steffi, I mean. Never having had a family, she must seem like a miracle for Nick.'

'Exactly,' Bill said, and must have sounded bleak for Kirsten put an arm around her shoulders.

'It *is* good, isn't it—for Nick, I mean?' she probed, and Bill assured her it was.

'I'm just overtired,' she said. 'How you manage kids and work I'll never know.'

She thought she'd sounded okay but the wondering look on Kirsten's face told her she'd failed.

'Well, look after yourself,' Kirsten said, giving Bill a hug. 'And if you need to talk to anyone, remember I'm not the family gossip.'

Bill had to smile for it was Bob's wife Jackie who claimed that title. Kirsten was the last person in the family to repeat anything told to her in confidence.

Nick found himself scowling at Rob Darwin every time they crossed paths that evening, but as the flow of ambulances was reduced to a trickle and the patients he was treating only had minor injuries, he had time to consider the situation more rationally. He knew he should be glad the man was interested in Bill because he himself certainly had no proprietorial rights on her, no claim at all, in fact.

And he definitely shouldn't be kissing her, for all his mind *and* body were obsessed by her.

Perhaps obsessed wasn't the word. Surely he couldn't

be *obsessed*? Obsessed drew pictures of stalkers and serial killers in most people's minds—

'You all right?' his patient asked, and he knew he must have groaned.

'Fine, just a long night. And you'll be fine too. Just remember to check the coverings on the wounds every day and if you start getting some yellowish seepage, come back here or see a GP.'

'I'll definitely come back here,' the patient said, and for the first time Nick registered that she was a very attractive young woman. English, from her accent, and though her long blonde hair was matted with blood and her face streaked with grime, he knew she'd clean up into something special.

He smiled at her, hearing Bill's voice whispering *Cradle-snatcher* in his head.

'You do that if you need to,' he said in his most professional voice, knowing it was highly unlikely she'd be back while he was on duty. One more night then he could take some time off and sort out a workable arrangement for himself and Steffi.

The thought of her brought a half-smile to his face and he realised again that, whatever lay ahead, giving Steffi a stable, happy life had to be his number-one priority.

Once Bill shifted out, it would be easier to work out what to do next. Easier to stop thinking about her as well.

It had to be.

He looked around the ER. The place had gone from chaotic to all but empty, only one sad drunk sitting on a bench and Nick had been told the man was homeless and often spent the night in the ER.

Had *he* ever had a family?

Surely not, for wouldn't a family have kept him sane and safe and off the streets?

Although not all families worked...

'Mine will,' he muttered.

And was startled when a passing nurse said, 'Your what will what?'

He grinned at her.

'Sign of advancing age, talking out loud,' he said, then realised the nurse in question was Amanda, the woman who'd asked him to join her and her friends on a trip to the islands. 'Oh, by the way, I won't be able to make it at the weekend—unexpected complications.'

'Old friend Bill more than just an old friend?' Amanda asked, surprising Nick so much he had no time to retort before she added, 'Hospital gossip machines work just as well in the country as in the city, and everyone in the ER has seen the way you look at her.'

He had to quash this right now! More for Bill's sake than for his.

'I've known Bill since we started school together in the kindergarten class, what's more—' like some pathetic loser about to tell a lie, he found himself crossing his fingers behind his back '—the gossip I've heard links her with a certain other doctor—one who was in here earlier.'

He walked away before he got himself deeper into the mire, sorry he'd had to implicate Bill in a relationship that didn't exist but not wanting to explain his current situation.

Not that he could explain it because he had no idea exactly what it was—apart from a disaster.

Although Steffi wasn't a disaster and if he concentrated on getting life right for her, then everything else should fall into place.

Or so he hoped.

He arrived home to find his friend and his daughter both dressed for the beach.

'She loves the bath so much I thought I'd try her in the pool—there's a paddling pool beside the big pool and the water in it is quite warm. But I thought it best to go early before the sun gets too hot. Here, you can have a little play with her before you head to bed and I'll put the washing on.'

Bill handed Steffi to him and walked away, and though he wanted to watch, he didn't, turning his full attention on his daughter, who was gurgling with delight, hopefully because she was pleased to see him.

'We'll manage on our own, won't we?' he said, lifting her high into the air. 'Just one more night with Bill then it's you and me against the world, kid,' he added, while she laughed down into his face.

He hugged her close, reaffirming the fact that she was more important than anything else in the world right now, and getting their lives together sorted out had to be his first priority.

So why the hell, when Bill returned, did he suggest he grab a coffee and some toast and join them at the pool?

Because he wanted to see with his own eyes how his daughter took to the water?

Or he wanted to see Bill in a bikini again?

Ridiculous—that was tempting fate and the look Bill gave him told him she thought so too, but he excused himself by deciding he didn't want to miss Steffi's first dip in a pool and hurried to fix some breakfast so he could join them.

Hell! She could do without seeing Nick with no shirt on. Didn't he realise they had to be seeing less of each other, not more?

Bill brooded on this as she and Steffi went down in the lift, exiting on the ground floor and walking out the back of the foyer to a beautifully landscaped recreation area. The two pools, formed so they looked like natural rock pools, were set in lush tropical vegetation. To one side was an outdoor barbeque and picnic space, tables and chairs set up beneath palm-fronded shelters.

On the other side was a long, narrow lap pool for serious swimmers, but for now all she and Steffi needed was the paddling pool.

Steffi saw the water and began to clap, making Bill realise she wasn't new to pools. Of course, her mother's New York apartment building could be modern enough to have one on site, probably on the roof.

Her mother.

Serena.

Just keep the beautiful blonde in the forefront of your mind when those abs come into view, Bill told herself, dropping their towels on a nearby chair, putting a little more sunscreen on Steffi's face then carrying her towards where the pool sloped from ankle depth to probably shoulder depth on Steffi.

The little girl paddled happily on the edge, splashing water up at Bill and chortling her delight.

'The notes said she's had swimming lessons.'

The abs had arrived, although right now they were decently covered by a T-shirt.

'I must have missed that part but lessons or not, you can't take your eyes off them for a minute around water,' Bill replied, then felt foolish and added, 'But of course you'd know that. I think child drownings are among the cruellest things we see in the ER.'

'Well, that's put a dampener on the fun, hasn't it, Steff?' Nick sat down in the water with his daughter and squirted water in his fists to make fountains.

She squealed with delight and once again he felt his heart fill with happiness. Whatever he had to sacrifice to give her the best possible life, he would. Not that resisting his attraction to Bill could be regarded as a sacrifice when they hadn't got past the kissing stage!

'One kiss does not a relationship make,' Bill said quietly, and he knew that once again their ability to follow each other's thoughts was in play.

'You are so right,' he told her. 'Now, how about you take over here while I swim about a hundred laps to convince my body of that?'

Bill laughed, which suggested that everything would be okay between them, but he knew it wouldn't—not unless they saw as little as possible of each other between now and when Serena returned. And, no, he told himself, he wasn't going to question the ethics of going back to Serena for the sake of his daughter—it was the right thing to do and he would do it.

Swim first, then sleep then one more night on duty, after which he'd get his new life organised...

How could so much have been organised while he slept?

Nick woke at two in the afternoon to find a note that

informed him his daughter was at playgroup, whatever that might be, and would be home at two-thirty. Two nannies were coming for interviews, Anna at four-thirty and Dolores at five-thirty.

Dolores? Who was called Dolores these days?

It had to be a measure of his overall confusion that he was spending precious brain power, limited right now, on an unknown person's name.

He showered, glanced around the apartment to make sure it was tidy then phoned Bob, who put him onto the right car dealer for the vehicle he'd decided would be safest for Steffi.

CHAPTER EIGHT

'AND JUST WHERE have you been?'

Bill was obviously angry when she greeted him just inside the door of the apartment when he returned at four twenty-five.

'I'm not late for the appointment,' he pointed out.

'No, but nervous would-be employees are usually early. Anna's sitting out on the deck with Steffi.'

Nick took in the faint flush of colour in Bill's cheeks and guessed the anger in her voice was more that of relief, the release of tension when someone had been worrying.

Over him, or the fact that he might miss the interview?

'I'd have phoned if I'd thought I'd be late,' he said, touching her gently on the forearm.

She stiffened immediately, then turned away, obviously not interested in the answer to her earlier question.

So he didn't tell her...

Why she'd let herself get all uptight over Nick being late, Bill didn't know. All she *did* know was that her relief at seeing him had prompted a surge of anger.

Stupidity, that's what it was!

She closed her eyes and prayed he'd like one of the

nannies enough to employ her and *she* could fade quietly into the background of his life.

This idea should have brought pleasure, but her visit to the playgroup with Steffi, seeing the other mothers and their children, watching Steffi's delight as she'd taken in the noise and colour, had brought back all the pain she'd suffered with the miscarriage, in her arms *and* in her heart.

'Plenty of small children around for you to play with,' she reminded herself, only to realise that since she'd come home after the miscarriage she'd deliberately avoided spending too much time with her smaller nieces and nephews. The older ones, yes, she regularly took them to the beach or went to watch their sporting fixtures.

But the infants—the toddlers...

'Would you two like tea or coffee?'

She called through the open door out to the deck, not venturing out because she didn't want to get involved.

Steffi looked up at her voice and left her hold on Nick's knee to stagger a couple of steps towards her, but Bill resolutely turned away.

Losing one child had been bad enough. To have this one worm her way any further into her heart then be lost to her—that would be too much.

She made the coffees, as requested, set the mugs on a tray, added biscuits and a fruit strap for Steffi and took the lot out on to the terrace.

'Aren't you joining us?' Nick asked.

Bill forced a smile as she replied.

'No, Anna and I had a good chat earlier.'

She fastened a bib around Steffi's neck and handed

her the treat, sitting her down on the tiled deck so she could eat it without smearing it all over the furniture.

'She seems a very placid child,' Anna said, and Bill found a better smile.

'She's the best,' she said, glad to be able to answer honestly. 'I suppose she's been used to so many different carers, she takes change for granted.'

Bill slipped away. While she'd been talking, Nick had leaned down and lifted Steffi onto his lap and the adoration on the little girl's face as she looked up at her father had nearly broken Bill's already badly damaged heart.

It's right they stay together, she told herself. It's how things should be.

But accepting the rightness of it did nothing to alleviate her pain.

Nick liked Anna and having read her references—all excellent—and seen her interacting with Steffi, he was certain she'd be the perfect nanny for his daughter. Because Bill had arranged another interviewee he would see her, too, but he felt more relaxed now he had at least one carer available.

'How do you see the hours working?' Anna asked. 'The agency explained you're a doctor who mainly does night duty, so would it be a live-in job?'

He studied the young woman, attractive enough, with a bright smile and a pleasant personality, then tried to picture her living with them—with him and Steffi—in the room Bill was using now—

'Look,' he said, feeling his way as another solution took vague form in his head. 'Originally, yes, I was employed to work in the ER and I told the hospital management that I'd be happy to do night shifts. Night shifts give you more time off—five nights on then three days off. In point of fact, it turns into four days off as they don't count the first day when you're supposed to catch up on the sleep you missed the previous night.'

Anna nodded but looked vaguely puzzled about where the conversation might be going.

'I should explain that I came back to Willowby largely to see more of my elderly grandmother, and the night shifts offered more opportunity to do things with her during the day. But now...'

Anna smiled.

'You're confused because you have to consider Steffi's needs as well, but in my opinion you'd still be better off doing night shifts. You get to see her in the morning when you come home, and in the afternoon. Depending on your timetable you could even eat dinner with her and put her to bed. Then on those days off you're all hers—or all hers and your grandmother's.'

'You're right,' Nick agreed, although in his gut he was still uncomfortable about the young woman sleeping here.

'How would you arrange your working hours if I stick to night duty?' he asked, throwing the onus of the decision back on her.

She considered it for a while, absentmindedly picking up another biscuit and eating it.

'I could start on the evening you begin duty and stay over for the five nights and days so you can sleep on your first day off. I'll be getting a meal for myself and Steffi so will do dinner for you each night, then when you're off duty I leave you in charge.'

It sounded okay but Nick still had misgivings.

'Is this the way nannying works? Do you not worry about living in a house with a man you barely know?

And doesn't if affect your social life? I mean, do you live at home or do you rent and if you rent, do you still have to pay rent if you're not there five nights a week?'

Anna smiled at him.

'Most employers don't give a damn about their nanny's social or financial life. In my case, I live with my partner—we've been together four years now. How I see it working is once Steffi's in bed and all my duties are done, with your permission and after you've met him, I'm sure my partner would be happy to visit.'

Uh-oh! Nick thought, imagining the two in the bedroom while Steffi screamed blue murder. Although wasn't there an intercom...?

'Not every night,' Anna continued, 'because he has his own interests, but occasionally he might bring over a DVD we can watch together. But that would only be with your permission. If you have any doubts, that's okay. You say the job's only temporary—that Steffi's mother is coming back—so I can survive a few weeks of not seeing my partner for five nights of the week.'

Nick felt reassured—mostly reassured. His sticking point still seemed to be the bedroom, which he now considered Bill's...

'You sound like a very sensible young woman and, being one, you probably realise the agency has sent two people for me to interview. I'll try to make up my mind by tomorrow morning and will be in touch either way.'

To Nick's surprise, because he'd been very impressed by Anna, Dolores won the nanny stakes hands down. An older woman, perhaps fifty, she was bright and vivacious and Steffi sank into her ample bosom and grabbed the chunky beads around her neck, obviously enamoured.

'No worry about the times you go or come, Doctor,' Dolores told him when he tried to explain the hours. 'I will be here for the little one. If you are here, I make myself scarce but can still make meals for you and her so you can spend more good time with her. She and I we do shopping, you write down what you like to eat. Money you pay for five nights I stay is more than enough for the week if you don't mind my living here even when not working. That way I can work a little bit—like a housekeeper as well as nanny. Nothing extra to pay.'

Nick knew he had to delve further and discovered Dolores's permanent home was with her son and his wife and family.

'This kind of job a nice holiday for me,' she told Nick. 'My grandchildren, five of them, and so wild, but being mother-in-law not my place to tell them how to behave so I have to keep mouth shut. I love them all, and they are good for me, but whew!'

She waved her hand in front of her face to indicate how tiring her grandchildren were.

Nick laughed, even more certain this woman would be the best possible nanny for his daughter.

He made arrangements about time and pay, aware he had to pay her through the agency. She played with Steffi for a while then carried her to the door, kissing both her cheeks before handing her back to Nick.

'I teach her a little Spanish,' she said. *'Adios, mi angelita.'*

Steffi waved a chubby hand, her gaze following Dolores as she headed for the lift.

'Well, kid?' Nick said to her, and Steffi crowed with delight.

Bill was in the kitchen, chopping vegetables, apparently for Steffi's dinner as the pile was varied but rather small.

'I thought we'd have grilled salmon and salad,' she said, without looking up. 'I'll do a lamb cutlet for Steffi but she can try the fish as well because she should be eating fish and it's not mentioned in the notes about what she eats and doesn't eat.'

Bill glanced up long enough to hand Steffi a piece of broccoli then turned her attention back to what must have been a really difficult carrot.

'So, she doesn't want to know about your new nanny,' Nick said to Steffi, who was munching on the broccoli.

Bill glanced up again, anxiety and something he couldn't read in her eyes.

'You've decided on one of those two?' she asked. 'There was one that will suit?'

Steffi slid out of his arms and crawled over to where her saucepan and wooden spoons were left on the floor, so Nick could turn his full attention on Bill, who sounded even more anxious than she looked.

'They were both great but Dolores wins hands down. She's older, which appeals to me, and she's obviously very used to children, and there was something motherly—or grandmotherly, I suppose—about her that won Steffi over from the start.'

'That's good,' Bill muttered, and turned her attention back to the carrot, though she did glance up to ask, 'Do you want to eat early with Steffi? If so, it might be an idea to turn on the barbeque to heat the grill plate. It's always better to cook fishy things outside because of the smell.'

Thus dismissed, Nick headed for the balcony, where the beauty of the view struck him afresh. He walked back inside, picked up his daughter, took Bill by the hand and led her outside.

'Isn't it great?' he said. 'And smell the sea.'

The sun was setting behind the building so the water was washed with pink and streaked with gold, the islands nothing more than purple lumps along the far horizon.

He put his arm around Bill's shoulders, as he must have done a thousand times in the past, and although she stiffened, he left it there.

'I thought you'd be pleased to be free of looking after me and Steffi,' he said quietly to his friend, resolutely ignoring the cries of his body that it wanted more than friendship.

'I would never want to be free of our friendship and I would hate to not be some small part of Steffi's life,' Bill said carefully, after a silence that had stretched too long.

Nick hugged her close, a friend hug.

'Daft woman!' he said. 'As if you'd ever be free of the two of us. You're our best friend, remember?'

Bill eased away from him, kissed Steffi's cheek and headed back indoors.

'Unfortunately, I do,' she said as she disappeared.

Nick set Steffi down with some toys Bill had left on the deck, and turned on the grill plate on the barbeque. He knew Bill was hurting, but why, he wasn't sure. There was the sudden eruption of attraction between them. It was mind-bogglingly strange, and with the advent of Steffi, definitely inconvenient, but they were both mature adults, they could resist attraction.

Couldn't they?

Of course they could, Bill probably better than him for she was a strong woman.

But there was something more, some pain he—
Steffi!

He'd been in New York when Bill had let him know
the wedding was off. So Steffi must be much the same
age as her child would have been and here he was, accepting her help, relying on her to look after Steffi when
every time she looked at the child she must feel pain
stabbing into her heart.

How stupid could one man be?

Not that there was much he could do about it now,
but Dolores was starting work in a couple of days...

They ate their early dinner on the deck, Steffi finding salmon very tasty.

'I'll clean up while you bath her and yourself,' Bill
said, and though Nick longed to talk to her, to say he
understood and to apologise for the pain he must unwit-
tingly have caused her, he knew now wasn't the time.
He'd be too rushed and, anyway, how could he put his
thoughts and emotions into words?

Bill watched the pair depart for the bathroom and
sighed. She stared at the after-dinner debris and sighed
again.

'Get a grip!' she finally muttered to herself, and she
stood up and began to stack the dishes on a tray.

It was great that Nick had found a good nanny, even
better that she could get out of his apartment. Then
this—surely you couldn't call it love-sickness—would
pass and her life would return to normal.

Or something approaching normal anyway...

She stacked the dishwasher, cleaned up the kitchen,
put away all Steffi's toys and seriously considered getting into bed and pulling the covers over her head, possibly for a year.

Although it would be better to do that in her own apartment, rather than Nick's.

And she certainly shouldn't be thinking bed and Nick in conjunction like that because it reminded her of all that could never be...

Giving up on the bed idea she went back out onto the deck. The lights from the marina at the base of the building lit up the neighbouring area, but the sea was a deep, dark navy and the distant islands nothing more than black shadows.

The familiar view, even seen from this height, soothed her troubled mind and eased the ever-present ache in her heart. She could almost smile at her stupidity because being attracted to one's unavailable best friend had to top the stupidity list.

'Steffi's asleep and I've set the baby monitor.'

Nick's voice came from behind her and she didn't turn, although when he slid his arms around her waist and held her lightly, she leaned back against him—yes, stupidity again but didn't she deserve *something*?

'I've been totally insensitive, letting you take over Steffi's care,' Nick said, his voice gruff as if this weird conversation he'd just begun was affecting him deeply. 'I didn't know what you'd been through but that's no excuse. I just let you step in without even considering how it would affect your life.'

Bill turned to face him, distancing herself by putting her hands on his shoulders and stepping back so she could look into his face.

'*What* are you talking about? I was happy to step in—in fact, I took it all on myself. You didn't have much say in it. So why are you wallowing in guilt?'

Nick studied her for a moment, as if trying to read

something in her face, and just standing there, looking at him looking at her, Bill knew it was more than attraction she was feeling for this man.

It was love.

'Steffi must be the same age as your baby would have been,' Nick said, pulling her close again into a warm hug—a *friendly* hug! 'It must hurt you just looking at her.'

Bill pushed away again and shook her head.

'And this is worrying you now when I'm about to be replaced?' she teased, then she became the hugger and Nick the huggee. 'Of course I look at Steffi and wonder what if, but having her to play with, to care for has been sheer joy, so enough of the guilt trip. Just get yourself off to work so you can afford to pay the nanny, not to mention kindergarten fees, swimming lessons, school fees...'

Nick stopped her teasing with his hand across her mouth and the kiss she pressed against his palm was as automatic as breathing.

The hand stayed there for an instant, then Nick turned and walked away, saying, over his shoulder, 'And that's a whole other problem, isn't it?' in a voice edged with what sounded like anger, although it could just as easily have been frustration.

Isn't it just, Bill sighed to herself.

CHAPTER NINE

DOLORES HAD FITTED so well into his and Steffi's life that Nick found himself, as his next days off drew close, wondering if he should consider some social activities. Amanda had mentioned a party and Bob had invited him to some big do at the yacht club. Bill, who hated boats because they moved so much, was unlikely to be there.

Bill.

She'd moved the few things she'd had with her out of his apartment on the day Dolores had moved in, and although Dolores obviously saw her—Miss Bill says this, Miss Bill says that, she would report to Nick in the evenings—Nick hadn't set eyes on her.

He knew from an occasional scribbled note on a patient chart that she must be working the day shift in the ER, but their paths hadn't crossed.

Should he call her?

He knew he should, if only to say thank you for all she'd done, but if he called, he couldn't trust himself not to ask to see her, and as she was obviously distancing herself from him, that would be unfair.

Although he *really* would like to know if she was finding this separation as difficult as he was. Did she think about him all the time, catch glimpses of someone she thought was him in the distance, only to be disappointed? Did she think about the kiss and find her body heating as she remembered?

Sitting at his desk in the little alcove he'd set up as a home office, he leaned his elbows on the desk and clasped his head in his hands.

And groaned!

'Dinner, Dr Nick,' Dolores called, and he pulled himself together and went through to the kitchen, where Steffi was already in her high chair, a lolly-pink bib around her neck, her chubby hands banging spoons on the tray.

'Nice bib, kid,' Nick said, and she crowed with delight.

'Miss Bill gave it to her.' Dolores straightened the bib, showing the giraffe appliquéd on it, then brushed her hand on Steffi's hair. 'Didn't she, sweetie?'

Dolores set a plate of meat and vegetables in front of Nick then sat down to feed Steffi. He'd learned by now that Dolores preferred to eat later but always made sure he and Steffi ate together.

The meal was delicious—all Dolores's meals were delicious—but this evening it failed to distract him from thoughts of Bill—Miss Bill, as Dolores insisted on calling her.

He'd thought, once their cohabitation had stopped, that the ache of desire that had been there in her presence would disappear, but, no, it simply grew stronger.

Work and Steffi, all he had to do was concentrate on those two things and surely, eventually, the attraction would die a natural death. People talked about unrequited love, but this was simply unfulfilled desire, a completely different animal.

'And we were at the mall so I didn't get the mail today.'

Dolores had finished feeding Steffi and was stacking dirty dishes in the dishwasher when Nick caught up with her conversation.

'If you don't want to collect it on your way to work,' Dolores continued, 'I will get it tomorrow.'

How could anyone be thinking of mail?

Nick smiled to himself at this totally inappropriate thought. He simply *had* to get his mind off Bill.

'I'll get it on my way out,' he assured Dolores, although it would mean stopping in the foyer on his way down to the basement car park.

It also meant he just happened to run into Rob Darwin, who was stepping into the lift as Nick exited.

They exchanged nothing more than courteous good evenings, but Nick knew someone in the building must have let Rob in and what were the chances that three people living here knew him?

Nick opened his mail box, emptied it, and tucked all the mail under his arm while he relocked the box. Given his mood, it was probably inevitable that the one piece of mail that slid to the floor was a postcard with a picture of the Statue of Liberty on it.

Refusing even to read it, Nick thrust it back in with the rest and went down to the basement.

Work didn't help. For a start he kept picturing Bill there, buzzing around with her quiet efficiency, always anticipating his needs when he had a tricky patient.

And when he wasn't picturing her there he was picturing her out with Rob Darwin, dining across a candlelit table from him, her hand touching his, just casually at first.

Would they park by Sunrise Beach on the way home?

His gut churned at the thought and by the end of his shift it took all his strength of mind to not knock on Bill's door when he got back to the apartment building the next morning, just to see how she looked...

And check whether Rob Darwin was there?

No!

He went directly to his apartment, showered, played with Steffi, ate the French toast Dolores cooked for him, and went to bed, certain that in sleep he'd lose the torment of his mind and body.

They were at Woodchoppers, Bill in a lime-green bikini, a colour that seemed incongruous until she slid into the water and the bikini apparently disappeared, melding in with the colour of the water so her sleek, slim body, rolling slowly over in the tiny waves, appeared naked.

Then he was in the water with her, both of them naked, swimming together in some way, bodies touching, arms pulling in unison through the water, Bill's body fitting into his, made to fit into his, her back moulded to his chest, the water cool, his blood on fire.

She turned and lay before him, offering herself up to him, but he didn't take her, simply looked, drinking in the riotous red hair, the pale pink of her lips, the tips of her breasts, as pink as her lips. He leaned closer to lick them, first one then the other, while she smiled to hide the trembling of her body.

Slim waist and flaring hips, more red curls, a nest that tempted his fingers, but he needed to know her better, to trace the contours of her body, feel the satin tex-

ture of her skin, kiss the little freckle just there at the
base of her neck and now, a desire prolonged too long,
taste again the sweetness of her lips.

Honeyed sweetness, moist warmth within, Bill no
longer passive, stirring beneath him, raising her hips
so her body slid against his—slid into place—to where
it was made to be.

Drifting now, entwined, their bodies one, but the
water failed to cool the fire that raced through his
blood and burned along his nerves—the fire of need,
of want—the urgency of desire.

He'd take her, she was his after all, part of him, the
better part. They'd reached the rocks, soft rocks, and
there he rolled her so she lay along his body, her breasts
crushed against his chest, kissing him with a passion
that told him the fire was in *her* blood as well, burning
along *her* nerves...

He rolled her beneath him, touched her face, brushed
back the burnished hair, smoothed his fingers over the
lightly tanned skin that stretched across her cheekbones.
Kissed her eyelids, kissed her nose, kissed the indenta-
tion beneath her pink ear, then lost himself once more
as her lips parted, begging for a kiss.

For more than a kiss?

Of course for more. She was his, he was hers, it had
to be—

Had he groaned aloud that he woke to the agonised
sound reverberating around his bedroom?

That he woke up and sat, sweating, shivering, cursing
now that he'd regressed to adolescence and the steamy
dreams of youth, though Bill had never been part of
those?

He clambered out of bed, aware he was alone from

the silence in the apartment, and headed for the shower, letting the water cascade over him, trusting it to wash away the memory.

Dreams faded, didn't they? Disappeared soon after waking, leaving nothing but ephemeral fragments too fine for memory to grasp?

Not this dream.

CHAPTER TEN

'You look fantastic!' Rob said when Bill collected him from his apartment near the hospital.

'Thank you,' she said, enjoying the compliment—stupidly pleased because, guessing her brother had also asked Nick, she'd made an extra effort, even straightening her hair so it hung like a shining dark red curtain down past her shoulders. 'But just remember I'm taking you there so you can meet some people outside the hospital circle. This is not a date.'

'Yes, ma'am.' Rob saluted as he said it, adding, with a wry smile, 'And I'll try to hide my broken heart.'

'Piffle,' Bill retorted, 'I bet you're so used to women falling at your feet, I'm nothing more than a novelty because I haven't.'

'Not *that* many women have fallen at my feet,' Rob argued, but he grinned as he said it and Bill had to hide a rueful sigh.

How simple it would have been to have fallen at Rob's feet—or even fallen just a little in love with him. How easy and uncomplicated. He was attractive, attentive, intelligent and had a good sense of humour—what more could a woman want?

But, no, she had to do the unthinkable, and for some

perverse reason fall in love with her totally unavailable
best friend.

This time the sigh must have escaped for Rob, who'd
been opening the car door for her, said, 'You're not re-
gretting asking me to this do, are you? Do you not usually mix with the local social crowd?'

Bill slid in behind the wheel.

'As a lot of the local social crowd are related to me
I can't avoid mixing with them, but as family, not at
things like this. But, no, I don't regret asking you, it
will be fun, beginning with the shock on my various
sisters-in-laws' faces when I walk in with a handsome
man who absolutely none of them know.'

Rob came round the car and sat beside her.

'Good,' he said. 'Let's both have fun!'

'Fun?' she muttered to herself ten minutes later.

Had she been out of her mind?

She didn't even have time to register her family's
reactions to her presence, because the first person she
sighted was Nick.

Nick, looking superb, in light-coloured slacks, a
white open-necked shirt and a grey jacket that would
probably exactly match his eyes.

Nick, talking to the leggy blonde they'd seen at
breakfast that first morning—

Amy someone?

Nick, raising an eyebrow, nothing more, as he took
in Rob by her side.

Glad she'd spent a fortnight's salary on the slinky
white dress that showed off her curves as well as her
tan, Bill led Rob into the throng, introducing him to
friends and relations, assuring him he didn't need to
remember names, finally finding Kirsten's sister, Sally,

a stunning brunette, who was currently single, having recently discovered the man she'd thought she loved was married.

'Sally, this is Rob, a friend from the hospital. He's new in town so would you be a darling and look after him for me while I do the rounds of the brothers who are here? If I talk to one and not another, they get all precious.'

Sally whisked Rob off to get a drink, and Bill, aware she had to drive home—with or without Rob—took a glass of sparkling mineral water from a passing waiter and slid towards one of the open doors that led onto a narrow deck overlooking the boats in the yacht club marina.

Straight hair and a slinky dress hadn't cut it when it came to armour against Nick. Just seeing him had made her stomach somersault, leaving her so shaken it had taken all her strength to smile and nod and talk until she'd found an opportunity to hand Rob to someone else and escape while she collected her emotions.

She breathed deeply, taking in the salt-laden air, listening to the clinking of the ropes and fastenings on the boats as they moved in their moorings, gazing upwards at the star-filled sky.

Now think!

Obviously if she was going to have this kind of physical reaction every time she saw Nick, she had to take steps to *not* see him. They'd remained friends through long separations so if one or other of them left town, surely they could revert back to their platonic relationship?

She could get a job anywhere and maybe it was time to move on. She'd come home to lick her wounds after the Nigel debacle and the loss of the baby she'd never had, but she was fine and fit and strong once again.

Apart from a little heart-sickness, love-sickness, whatever—but work could cure that. Challenging work—something different, a foreign country, somewhere she'd be needed—

'I think your boyfriend's fallen hard for Sally— surely there was a less attractive woman you could have left him with?'

Nick was right behind her, so close she could feel the heat of him, smell his aftershave.

'He's just what Sally needs,' Bill answered, refusing to turn round because if hearing Nick's voice made her feel so uptight, then seeing him would probably paralyse her completely. 'He's nice and uncomplicated and funny and definitely not married.'

'I'm not married,' Nick said, his voice tight, strained, husky with emotion.

'No, but you have a family you can't betray so it's the same thing.'

Bill had done her best to keep *her* voice light and even, but the words had come out in a pathetic, wimpy kind of wail.

It was because he was so close—so close and yet not touching. Her nerve endings were reaching out towards him, straining against her skin so it was tight and hot— wanting to feel him, to be held, to lose herself in—

She stepped closer to the railing, hoping to break the bond that wasn't there.

Refocussed on her thoughts.

Maybe—

'Will you go back to live in Sydney?'

The 'when Serena returns' hung, unspoken, in the air.

Nick didn't reply, the silence stretching so long Bill wondered if he would, but when he did speak she knew it was something he'd been considering already.

'I want to stay here, Bill. I owe it to Gran, and also, now there's Steffi, I think I'd like her to grow up here. Serena has always worked out of Sydney, but these days she's in demand all over the world so I can't see why she couldn't be based here as well. She's Steffi's mother, Bill, for all her bizarre behaviour, and I'm sure, in her own way, Serena must love her daughter. Mother, father, child—that's a family, isn't it?'

'Exactly what you wanted,' Bill reminded him. 'But you should at least *try* to sound pleased about it.'

'How can I?' came the anguished cry, then his arms looped around her waist and he pulled her back so she was held against him, her body fitting his as neatly as two matching pieces of a puzzle. 'Damn it, Bill, how could this have happened? And why now, when it's impossible? Was life meant to be this way? One disaster after another?'

Bill rested her head against his shoulder and looked up at the sky.

Play it lightly, she told herself, although she knew the rapid beating of her heart beneath his hands would have already given her away.

'Melodrama, Dr Grant?' she teased. 'You can hardly label Steffi a disaster. More a miracle, and a delightful, gorgeous miracle at that. As for us, well, that would probably never have worked, even if we'd given in to the attraction. We know each other too well—there'd have been no mystery to keep the buzz alive.'

She was doing really well, she thought, until he lifted her hair and kissed the nape of her neck, sending a violent shudder of desire right through her body. And if her heart had been racing earlier, it now went into overdrive, hammering against her chest, while she could feel the moisture of her need between her thighs.

'Say that again—the bit about it not working,' Nick murmured against her skin, but Bill was beyond speech, beyond thought or voluntary movement. She let Nick hold her, let him kiss his way along her shoulder, let his hands roam across her breasts, thumbs teasing at her traitorously peaking nipples.

She grabbed the railing, no longer trusting her legs to hold her up as her bones melted under the onslaught of Nick's touch.

A sudden gust of wind, a louder rattle in the rigging of the yachts and she came thudding down to earth.

'For heaven's sake, Nick, we're practically in public!' she growled, trying to twist out of his grasp but only succeeding in turning to face him.

'So, where can we be private? Your place?'

Now she pushed away, shaking her head, hoping like hell she wasn't going to cry.

'You don't mean that, Nick, I'm sure you don't. Mother, father, child—family, remember? If you were to betray that then you're not the man I've always thought you, and certainly not the man I love.'

She spun away, heading not back inside but down the steps at the end of the balcony towards the marina itself. The 'l' word had come out without censorship but hopefully he'd take it as friend love not lover kind of love. Rob would have to fend for himself because there was no way she could go back inside and face family and friends with any kind of composure.

The tears she refused to shed were banked up behind

her eyes and she knew from the heat in her cheeks that they'd be fiery red.

With anger, frustration or pain?

She had no idea. All she knew was that her feelings for Nick had strayed so far beyond the realms of friendship that she would *have* to get away.

Nick wanted to follow her but knew he couldn't. Knew also he'd have to stay out on the balcony a little longer while the raging desire in his body cooled and he could face the crowd with some semblance of control.

She was right, of course. Even thinking about the things he'd like to do with Bill was a betrayal of sorts, but how could he face Serena with the suggestion of family if he'd physically betrayed her?

He thumped his fist against the railing, which did nothing more than hurt his hand, and was relieved when he heard a voice behind him—Amy joining him on the balcony.

'I thought I'd lost you,' she said. 'Boy, it's a crush in there. You didn't say if you're interested in a trip to Hayman Island on your next days off. I'm working as a boat hostess out there now and can get you a good deal on accommodation, and there's a huge party for the launch of some new perfume going on all week.'

'Thanks, but, no, thanks,' Nick said, but inside his gloom lifted just a little as he realised how much one small person had changed his life. A couple of days on a tropical paradise had no appeal whatsoever when set against a couple of days playing with Steffi.

Perhaps he wouldn't always feel like this, but right now the more he got to know his daughter, the more fascinating he found her.

So fascinating he found himself explaining his refusal.

'Steffi's going to walk on her own any day now, and I'd hate to miss seeing her take off.'

Amy laughed and shook her head.

'I gathered when you were talking about her earlier that she'd won you over, but to hear Playboy Nick refusing a gala party to see a baby take her first steps, that beats everything.'

She studied him for a few moments before adding, 'So it means you and Serena will get back together?'

'I'm assuming so,' Nick replied, ignoring the cold lump that formed in his stomach as he spoke.

'Well, that *will* be interesting,' Amy said with a smile he couldn't quite fathom. He hadn't liked the emphasis on the 'will' either but she disappeared back into the party before he could ask what she meant.

But at least now he could leave without worrying he'd run into Bill either in the marina car park or the building basement. The less he saw of Bill the better.

'Oh, Doctor Nick, I was going to phone you but Miss Bill arrived with the spade just in time. The little one, she was making an awful noise with breathing but Miss Bill has her in the en suite and she's okay now.'

Bill arrived with a spade?

Nick was striding towards his bedroom but that bit of the garbled conversation kept repeating itself in his head.

He opened the door to a fog of steam, a bedraggled-looking Bill sitting on the lavatory seat with Steffi asleep on her knee.

No spade.

'Croup!' Bill said as Nick bent over his daughter, automatically feeling for a pulse, listening to her breathing. 'Dolores said she opened the air-conditioning vent in Steffi's room because she was restless when she went to bed. If she has a bit of a cold, the cool, dry air could have caused the croup.'

Bill was talking sense, he knew that, but his medical brain was telling him that sudden stridor in a child's breathing could be caused by an inhaled foreign object.

'She's breathing normally now.' Bill answered his doubts as he lifted Steffi into his arms and held her tightly against him. 'I think she can go back to bed. I asked Dolores to turn off the air-conditioning earlier and although humidifiers are rarely needed up here in the tropics, it might be advisable to have one on hand for those hot nights when Steffi might need air-conditioning in her room.'

Nick looked down at Bill, at the hair beginning to regain its curl, at the damp dress clinging to her figure...

No, he wouldn't look there.

'We never had it, did we?'

Bill met the question with a puzzled frown.

'Had what?'

'Air-conditioning, you dope.'

That won an almost normal Bill smile.

'Never knew it existed outside of supermarkets and shopping malls. Remember how packed the malls were on really hot days?'

'Malls, hospitals and court houses,' Nick recalled, while relief flooded through him that he and Bill hadn't lost their easy, casual friend-type conversation.

Relief that vanished when she stood up and he remembered his dream when the lime-green bikini had apparently disappeared. The white slinky dress was in danger of doing the same thing and in his mind he saw her standing there naked in front of him.

His heart stopped beating, his breathing arrested, the world stood still and silent as he simply gazed at the woman he couldn't have.

'Put Steffi to bed—or maybe into your bed,' she said, breaking the spell so his organs resumed their normal function. 'That way you'll hear her if her breathing becomes hoarse.'

She smiled at him then—a lovely, cheeky Bill grin—and added, 'I bet that's one you haven't thought about yet. Is the kid allowed to sleep in your bed from time to time?'

He hadn't, but neither had he ever thought he'd feel anything other than the love of friendship for Bill, although right now, in this steamy bathroom, he began to suspect that was exactly what had happened.

Escaping was the obvious thing to do and he had the perfect excuse—putting Steffi to bed. The steam had made her clothes damp and she'd need a dry nappy. He'd do that—change her—now...

'I can't get out with you blocking the doorway,' Bill complained, but a tremor in her voice suggested that she, too, was feeling the tug of desire that had come from nowhere to confuse them.

The tug of love?

Had she said 'love' earlier?

'Move!' she ordered, remaining where she was, not coming close enough to push him out the door.

Not wanting to touch him for fear of where it might lead?

He moved, carrying Steffi through to her bedroom,

assuring Dolores the little girl was all right, reassuring himself at the same time.

A small red plastic spade was lying on the floor beside Steffi's cot. Having dug with it himself when he'd taken his daughter to the beach, he now understood the earlier conversation.

Dolores, who followed him in, picked it up and set it in the box of toys.

'Miss Bill found it in the lift and knew it was Steffi's,' she explained, then she burst into tears, falling over herself as she apologised again and again.

'Dolores, I would have turned on the air-conditioning,' Nick said very firmly. 'No one is blaming you. Now, go and have a cup of tea or a drink of whatever you need. I'm home and I'll take care of her tonight so shift the monitor into my room and get a good night's sleep yourself.'

But Dolores didn't move, repeating all she'd said, apologising tearfully over and over again until Bill appeared, put her arm around the older woman's shoulder and led her away.

Steffi, woken by the noise or by having her clothes changed, looked up at Nick and smiled sleepily. His heart filled with joy and as he bent and kissed her belly button he knew she had to come first in his life, her welfare, her physical and emotional development the most important things in his life.

The thought brought pain but better he suffer than she grow up with parents fighting for her. Mother, father, child—a family...

Bill sat in the kitchen, pouring a little rum into the cup of hot chocolate she'd made for Dolores, pleased the woman was finally calming down. But much as she,

Bill, wanted to leave—to escape before she had to face Nick again—she couldn't leave an even half-hysterical woman on his hands.

His attention had to be focussed on Steffi.

'It was a natural thing to do and of course Nick isn't going to fire you. You're the best thing that's ever happened to him and his daughter,' Bill repeated for about the eleventh time.

Dolores looked at her, her eyes red from weeping, her normally olive skin blotchy with emotion.

'You think so, Miss Bill?'

'I know so,' Bill said, and she leaned over and kissed the older woman on the cheek. 'Nick and Steffi couldn't do without you.'

'And when his wife comes back? He showed me postcard from New York.'

'Heaven only knows what will happen,' Bill told her, 'but I can't imagine you won't be part of their lives.'

Dolores smiled and Bill knew she could finally escape. Nick would stay with Steffi wherever she was sleeping.

Nick…

CHAPTER ELEVEN

TEN DAYS LATER Nick flew to Sydney with Steffi, Dolores and all the baby paraphernalia he now counted as normal baggage. Much as he hoped he and Serena could make a life in Willowby, he knew it would be easier to talk to her in her own apartment.

She'd had two days to get over any jet-lag she might be suffering, and although she hadn't sounded delighted when he'd told her they were coming, she hadn't objected.

Surely that had to be a good sign.

And she wasn't stupid, so she'd understand his argument that she could really be based anywhere...

'You worried, Dr Nick?' Dolores asked, as he drove the hire car he'd organised from the airport to Double Bay.

'No, Dolores,' he replied, although his gut was churning and every imaginable disastrous scenario was racing through his head.

The only scenario he hadn't imagined was finding Alex at the apartment—Alex cooing over Steffi, who obviously remembered him, while Serena barely acknowledged her child.

'Alex is here because he wants to photograph Australia,' Serena explained, and while Nick thought that might be a tall order, he refrained from comment. 'I didn't know you'd bring your nanny, she'll have to share with Steffi. I think the building manager has roll-out beds available.'

Nick had already fitted five people into three bedrooms in his head and realised Serena was assuming he would share her bed.

But wasn't that why he'd come?

To build the family that he wanted?

Mothers and fathers did share beds...

'I can sleep on the couch,' he heard himself say, when Alex, carrying Steffi, had led Dolores off to show her the bedroom they would use.

Serena studied him, eyebrows raised.

'Do you hate me so much, Nick?'

He shrugged, feeling awkward and uneasy because he didn't fully understand the situation himself.

'I don't hate you at all,' he said—at least that much was true. 'Yes, I was angry and upset over your deception but how could I hate you when you've given me Steffi? However, we're virtually strangers to each other. Not counting your brief visit to Willowby it's been eighteen months since we've seen each other—longer than that since we've been together.'

She smiled now.

'I doubt we've forgotten how to make love,' she murmured, moving closer so he knew he should take hold of her, feel her body against his—feel excitement, even.

Except he couldn't.

'I think we need to talk first, to work out where we're going.'

The smile faded from her face and it was her turn

to shrug. With all the elegance of her trade she moved away, over to the marble coffee table in the centre of the living room, bending to pick up a packet of cigarettes.

'You're not going to smoke with Steffi in the apartment!'

The words burst from his lips and he knew he must have spoken far too loudly because Serena spun towards him, more shock than surprise on her face.

'So now you're the smoking police,' she said, her voice tight. 'I remember *you* used to have a cigarette from time to time.'

The sly smile that crept across her face told him she knew her words had struck home, because occasionally, when she'd had a cigarette after sex, he'd had a puff or two—sharing hers, thinking of it as another kind of shared act...

He forced himself to remain calm.

'I'm sorry I reacted badly but Steffi's had a bad attack of croup and I've been worried about her lungs. Can we sit outside while you smoke?'

Serena nodded and led the way out onto the balcony. From here he could see glimpses of the harbour, the sun glinting off the water.

'The view from my apartment in Willowby has more water, but the harbour view is always magnificent,' he conceded.

'So, you could get used to it again?' Serena asked. 'We'd need to move to a bigger apartment because the nanny should have her own room and we'll always need a spare for visitors.'

This was it! This was where he had to say something.
But what?
And how?

How!

The word appealed to him. He knew her life, he'd work into it that way.

'How are your bookings looking? Where do you go next? Will you be mainly overseas?'

Serena squinted through a trail of smoke that curled up from her lips—lips that would kiss Steffi tasting of tobacco.

If she ever kissed Steffi…

'And you're asking why?'

Yes, Serena wasn't stupid. Self-focussed but not stupid.

He'd come to talk, Nick reminded himself. So talk.

'I think, ideally, Steffi needs both her parents. I realise your career is very important to you and I think she'd learn to live with the fact that you're often away, as long as she has stability in the rest of her life, like myself and Dolores—or whatever nanny we might employ.'

That sounded good so far, he congratulated himself while he waited for a comment from Serena.

'And?'

That was it? A one-word prompt, giving no indication of what she was thinking or feeling?

'As you know, I returned to Willowby to be close to Gran, to whom I owe so much. I think it would be a great place to raise a child, or children, and I wondered whether it mattered to you where you were based. If you're mostly flying out to assignments around the world, you could just as easily fly from there, not right away as you've obviously got this Australian trip planned, but after that?'

He'd made a mess of it, he could feel it in his bones, although Serena's face showed no emotion whatsoever.

Neither did she respond, simply putting out one cigarette and taking another one out of the packet, holding
it distractedly between her fingers.

'Well?' he finally asked, and hoped it hadn't sounded
like a demand.

'You've obviously been thinking about this for some
time,' she said, 'this fantasy of family. Yet you're not
willing to share my bed.'

So that was what had upset her!

You could fix that by agreeing—would it be so hard?
a voice in his head demanded.

The shiver that ran through his body—not distaste
but definitely uneasiness—gave him the answer.

'I think we should look at where we're going before
we leap into bed together,' he said. 'Sex rarely solves
anything—in fact, it probably makes situations more
complicated.'

'You've changed,' she said, and although he knew a
lot of the change was to do not with Steffi but with his
feelings for Bill, he had an easier answer.

'I think having a child changes everyone.'

'Maybe.'

Nick had to be satisfied with that enigmatic response
because Alex joined them on the balcony, still carrying
Steffi, who was playing with his beard.

'We could photograph the child in all the places we
spoke of,' he said to Serena. 'Ayers Rock and White-
haven Beach and in the snow.'

'No!'

Nick and Serena spoke together, Nick adding, 'Well,
at least we agree on something,' although he guessed
Serena's 'no' was for a different reason. She didn't want
Steffi stealing her limelight.

'Okay,' Alex said, accepting the judgement and setting Steffi down on the floor. 'And don't you dare light that cigarette and breathe smoke all over the child,' he added to Serena, who, to Nick's surprise, obediently put the offending object back into its box.

'So, the Australian photography, that's one project you've got lined up?' he said to Serena, grasping Steffi's hand as she pulled herself up on a chair and stumbled towards him. 'What's next?'

But Serena didn't answer. Standing up, she stepped carefully over Steffi and headed inside, the slamming of a door suggesting she'd taken refuge in her bedroom.

'I keep telling her not to smoke at all,' Alex complained, 'but she says it's all that keeps her from eating and that way she stays slim.'

He shook his head and followed Serena indoors, knocking cautiously on her bedroom door.

Nick swung Steffi onto his knee.

'Not going too well, is it, kid?' he said, then he kissed her neck and delighted in her baby smell and her warm chuckles.

But not for long!

He had four days to work something out with Serena, and although his head told him Willowby was the ideal place for his family, his heart suggested that staying in Sydney might be easier for a whole lot of reasons—not because it was definitely Serena's preference but because of the distance from Bill.

Bill tried not to think about what was going on in Sydney. She told herself she hoped Nick could work it out, but in her heart of hearts she hoped he'd work it out so they stayed in Sydney. He could fly up to visit Gran...

So life went on—going to work, coming home, doing everything she could to not think about Nick, although memories were everywhere, especially when she visited Gran, who talked so excitedly about Nick bringing Serena home to Willowby, about weddings and more babies, every word a drop of acid etching pain into Bill's heart.

Work provided, if not solace, a least a release from constantly thinking about Nick. It was impossible to let your thoughts drift in a busy ER.

'Bill, you're on the mine rescue team, aren't you?'

Angie had slid into the cubicle where Bill was dressing an elderly man's leg ulcer.

'Yes,' Bill replied, her mind on the job, thinking Angie might be asking because she was interested in joining the team.

'Then I'll take over there,' Angie said. 'There's an alert. An accident at Macaw.'

Bill's heart, which had stopped beating at the word 'alert', resumed when she heard Macaw mentioned. It was an underground mine and both her brothers now worked in open cuts.

As she left the cubicle the phone she carried in one pocket began to vibrate and she knew this would be the call asking her to report to Rescue Headquarters.

Her stomach clenched as she thought of what might have happened. All the mines had their own safety officers and trained rescue personnel, but the mine rescue team was called in for serious accidents—a roof collapse, miners trapped...

'It's what we've all trained for,' the team leader reminded the group as they kitted themselves out in overalls, breathing apparatus, hard hats with attached lights, and lethal-looking tools that could cut, or lever; with ropes and whistles and walkie talkies.

Emergency equipment was already being moved to the mine, including the huge jet engine that would pump inert gas in to smother explosive gases. She knew enough about underground mining to be aware of the safe-refuge chambers, where trapped miners could gather, and escape shafts equipped with ladders for them to escape. Gas was the big problem, gas that could explode into fire or poison people trapped beneath the earth.

'It's a rock fall, not a fire,' the team leader told them. 'And Macaw's got the latest in monitoring and communication equipment so by the time we get there they will know just how many and where the men are trapped.'

Bill thought of other mine disasters she'd read about or seen on TV and was glad about the communication because at least the men could talk to the outside world.

When the team arrived at the mine, the management had their rescue protocols under way and could tell them fourteen men were trapped, eleven in a safe-refuge chamber, only one miner that they knew of quite seriously injured.

'We've one team working on access to the chamber now, and another drilling a new ventilation shaft down to it. We think the other three men are further down that stope and we've men trying to get to them from an escape shaft.'

Knowing no one would have been allowed into the mine, even for a rescue mission, unless the air readings were good and the shafts secure, Bill felt a surge of hope that all the men would be rescued alive.

Maybe not today, but before too long.

* * *

In Sydney, Nick had renewed his conversation with Serena. Steffi was having a sleep and Alex had apparently calmed Serena down so she was willing to listen to him.

'We got on well before,' he reminded her. 'We really only broke up because your work took you away so often. I'm not asking you to stop work, only asking if you don't think, for Steffi's sake, we could make it work again.'

'In Willowby?' Serena demanded. 'I think not. I was only there for a few hours and the heat nearly killed me. Besides that, there's my social life. It's all right for you, you've friends up there, but all my friends are here or overseas.'

Nick wanted to point out that people's social lives changed as they grew older and had more responsibilities but knew that wouldn't cut any ice with Serena. They'd suited each other before because they'd matched—playboy and playgirl.

And he'd thought that life was fun?

'And Steffi?' he asked, as he'd yet to see any indication that Serena cared one jot for her child.

'She's my daughter.'

The shrug Serena gave as she answered made Nick want to shake her. She might not love her child but she was obviously willing to use her as a bargaining chip.

Or was she?

Was he just assuming that her blood tie was as strong as his?

'Do you want her?' he asked, and now Serena turned to face him.

'Why wouldn't I?' she demanded, and Nick threw up his hands in despair.

'I've no idea,' he said. 'Not about this, or you, or anything! According to what you told me earlier, you were willing to have her adopted as soon as she was born, then last month, when you had to fly to the States for work, you were apparently quite happy about dumping her on me, so what am I supposed to think?'

'You're supposed to understand I'm her mother,' Serena said, and Nick, his heart sinking, knew she saw Steffi as nothing more than a pawn in whatever game she was currently playing.

'And?' he prompted, not wanting to say too much, not wanting to let the anger building inside him loose anywhere near his daughter.

'That's all. You must realise that in family law disputes the judge almost always gives custody to the mother.'

'You're saying you want her?' Nick demanded, his stomach in knots at the thought of having a legal fight for his daughter. 'You want to be part of her life? Always, or just until she gets in the way of your career?'

Serena lit another cigarette from the stub of the one she'd just finished, and blew a lazy plume of smoke into the air.

'What do *you* want, Nick?' she asked, and Nick, although now he was wondering about it himself, answered her.

'I want us to be a family,' he said. 'I think that's the least we can do for Steffi. She didn't ask to be here, but now she is, let's see if we can give her the best possible life, which, to me, means two parents.'

'I only ever had my mother, and you had no one but your grandmother,' Serena reminded him.

'And look at the mess we both made of things,' Nick

snapped. 'Why do you think I want two parents for Steffi?'

'I won't accept such nonsense. I'm successful, you're successful, but I get your point, I just don't get living in that God-awful place up north. If you want to play happy families with me and Steffi, you'll have to play here.'

It would be best to be here, Nick conceded in his heart. Far away from Bill and the threat to his equilibrium that she now represented.

'There's Gran...' he muttered, but so tentatively Serena had no trouble laughing off his feeble objection.

'You could fly up twice a month to visit her,' she said. 'Even take the child.'

The child?

Was he wrong to be thinking of Serena as the mother figure in his family if she didn't love Steffi?

'Do you love her?'

The question erupted out of him—far too loud and far too abrupt.

Serena smiled the serene smile he knew she practised so it matched her name.

'I'm her mother, aren't I?' she responded, telling him absolutely nothing.

He slept on the couch, took Steffi for walks around traffic-busy streets, talked to Alex and Dolores, his life in limbo.

Because he wouldn't share Serena's bed?

He'd asked himself the question, suggested perhaps everything would fall into place once he did, but something held him back—something more than a few errant kisses up in Willowby. It came down, he decided, to Serena's attitude towards Steffi. She showed no interest in her child, never stopping to play with her, to touch her, to hold her in her arms and cuddle her.

And slowly it began to seep into his family-obsessed brain that perhaps the mother, father, child scenario wasn't all that it was cracked up to be. Well, he'd always known that, known the divorce statistics and the prevalence of single-parent families, so why had it seemed so important to him?

'I've booked a table at Fiorenze for tonight,' Serena announced, coming out onto the deck where he was watching Alex and Steffi build a tower of blocks. 'Alex and I are off tomorrow, so this will be our last chance to talk.'

'Tomorrow?' Nick repeated, looking from Serena to Alex, who simply shrugged.

'Tomorrow!' Serena repeated.

Nick knew he must look as stunned as he felt. The previous talk had been of a departure ten days away.

'You mean we've got one whole day in which to work out the rest of our lives?' he demanded.

'And one night,' Serena added, smiling in such a way he knew she'd planned this carefully. A candlelit dinner at a place where they'd eaten often in the past, then home, slightly tipsy, to fall into bed together.

Maybe it would work...

He'd barely had the thought when she added, 'You're more than welcome to stay on here—it would give you time to find us a bigger apartment.'

Nick closed his eyes and counted to ten, determined not to explode in front of Steffi. He realised now that Serena's mind had been made up from the start, which was why she'd cut off any discussion about their future.

For some obscure reason—just to have a man around?—
she wanted him back and was happy to have 'the child',
as she called her daughter, included in the package. Tonight, in Serena's mind, he'd fall back into her bed and
the matter would be settled.

She'd disappeared before he'd regained enough control to follow her and insist they talk—off to buy a new
dress for tonight, according to Dolores.

He slumped down on the couch, knowing he'd been
too weak, too tentative, trying to do what was best for
everyone without upsetting any of the parties.

Well, maybe not best for everyone but best for Steffi.

Sick of the chaos in his head he flicked on the television and stared blankly at the screen, only slowly coming to the realisation that every channel was showing
the same thing—a mine, miners trapped, mine rescue
teams already on site. The disaster was here in Australia—Macaw.

Macaw was near Willowby...

CHAPTER TWELVE

'DOLORES, PACK UP all Steffi's things, we're going home,' he yelled, beginning to stuff his own gear into his bag then realising he'd need to book a flight.

Impossible. Every journalist in Australia was trying to get to Willowby—

'Dolores, can you drive? Have you got a licence?'

'Of course, Dr Nick, you know that, but why, what is wrong?'

'We'll have to drive, no chance of a flight. We'll take turns and stop overnight somewhere on the way—we have to think of Steffi.'

Serena arrived home as he was stacking all their gear in the hall.

'What's this?'

'I'm going home—there's trouble—I'm needed there.'

She looked at him for a long moment then said, 'It's that woman Bill, isn't it? It's always been Bill!'

And on that note she stormed away, slamming the bedroom door for must have been the twentieth time since his arrival.

It wasn't until he was out of the city, on the freeway, heading north, that he had time to consider what Serena has said.

It's always been Bill!

Had it?

No, he was certain that wasn't the case. Until he'd come back to Willowby he'd never thought of Bill as other than a friend.

So why had the attraction flared so quickly?

'I don't know,' he muttered, waking Dolores up from a light doze then being unable to explain exactly what it was he didn't know.

Because Bill had done some of her training at Macaw and knew it well, and possibly because, in the stressed situation, the recue organiser didn't realise she was a woman, she was one of the two chosen to go down the escape shaft to follow the miners through to where the three missing men might be trapped.

Excitement and trepidation churned inside her as she followed her partner down the ladder. Her brother Dan had told her that the ladders were checked every day so although this one seemed to move away from the wall a little, she kept faith in it.

'Two more levels to go,' the miner at the bottom of the shaft told her, and Bill touched him on the shoulder in thanks and sympathy, knowing how much he must want to be doing more to help his mates but sticking to his job in the whole operation right there at the bottom of the ladder.

The next shaft was darker and they turned on their lights so it glowed like a vertical tunnel with a train coming through. One more shaft and they were on the level of the fall, bright lights ahead showing them where the men were working.

'We've opened up a small passage over the top of

this fall,' one of the miners explained, 'but we can't get the communication probe through.'

He looked at Bill, the least bulky of the four people in the shaft.

'Reckon you can crawl up there and push it through.'

'I'll just drop this gear,' she said, and ignored the 'Crikey, it's a woman' comment from the second miner, leaving her partner to explain she was one of the top members of the mine rescue team. Clad just in her overalls and with a tiny mike attached to her shirt just below the collar, she was ready.

One of the men hoisted her up and she clambered into the small space the men had cleared, slowly edging her way forward, following the fine metal tube that was the probe, glad to see bolts in the stone above her that told her the roof of this part of the tunnel was safe.

The going was so slow she sometimes wondered if she was moving at all, but eventually she could see the end of the thin wire.

The probe had stuck on a rock that projected from the wall and she had to manoeuvre the tube around it, and keep feeding it forward. The opening she was in grew narrower and she knew she wouldn't be able to follow the probe, but a shout as she pushed it further and further told her it had reached the trapped men.

Berating himself all the way, Nick drove north. How stupid had be been to think a family could work without love? How stupid had Bill been, too, now he came to think about it!

Berating Bill for her stupidity was easier than thinking of her endangering herself in a mine accident, or trapped underground, or—

He'd think of numbers. He could reach Brisbane in ten hours, twelve allowing time to stop and rest and eat and let Steffi have a run around. Another ten—or twelve—and he'd be home.

He pressed the speed dial on his phone for the fortieth time and got the out-of-range message from Bill's mobile. He thought of phoning Bob but common sense told him it was better he didn't know what Bill was doing—not while he was driving.

Dolores drove as calmly and competently as she did everything else so he could sleep while she was at the wheel.

It was tempting to keep driving but, no, working in the ER he knew too well the risk of an accident when driving for too long. They'd stop, eat, sleep and go on refreshed. Tomorrow they'd be home.

Home!

He didn't dare dwell on Bill, on where she was or what she might be doing, he just knew he had to be there, to be close to wherever she was…

Bill could hear the excitement in the voices ahead of her, but although their words would be clear to those at the other end of the communication probe, they were jumbled coming through the rock to her.

She tried to work out differences in the voices, certain there were two, but three? She wasn't so sure.

'I'm coming out,' she said into her mike and, carefully, she began to edge backwards, knowing there would probably be other things she'd have to shove through to the men. Squirming backwards over stones wasn't fun, and it took far longer than she'd taken going in. Time ceased to exist but in the end she managed, knowing she was almost out when someone caught hold of her boots then guided her feet to footholds on the rocks.

'All three safe,' one of the miners told her. 'You did good,' adding, 'for a girl,' but smiling as he said it—the smile a bigger thank you than words could ever express.

She sat now, knowing the rule to rest when you could, while the men listened to the probe and began to plan the next move.

'How big is the gap, do you think?'

Her rescue partner came to sit beside her and Bill replayed her journey in her head.

'There's a rock jutting out from the wall that had stopped the probe and from what I could feel with my hand in that area, there's maybe a gap the size of a small water pipe. Once I got the probe through there, it wasn't impeded in any way. It reached the men about a metre past that small gap.'

'Small water pipe?'

He shaped his fingers to show her the circumference he was imagining and she agreed he'd got it right.

'Could it be widened?'

Bill closed her eyes and looked at a mental image of the rock jutting out in the light from her helmet, at the rocks around it, one exceedingly large one right at the top.

'Not without a great deal of trouble,' she replied.

'Well, we'll make do with what we've got,' her partner said. 'You willing to go back in?'

'Of course, but if you're getting pipe sent down, get that flexible stuff that will bend a bit around obstacles. I can use a guide wire to push it through, like the one the probe had.'

Technicalities kept them busy, messages going back and forth for hours until it was time for Bill to crawl back into the narrow space again, this time pushing the pipe in front of her, the pipe that might prove a lifeline for the miners if they were trapped there for much longer.

He *had* to know!

Having spent the night in a motel just north of Brisbane, they were on the road again at dawn, and Nick finally cracked and turned on the radio. He knew Dolores would have watched the drama on the television in her room at times during the night, but he'd been resolute in not watching anything that might stop him sleeping.

'It is bad, Dr Nick,' Dolores said. 'It is why we're going home?'

'Yes.'

One word was all he could manage, the news that rescuers had reached the eleven men in the safe refuge should have cheered him, but it had been followed by the information that members of the mine rescue squad were three levels underground, still trying to get to the other three men, and that had dried the saliva in his mouth, certain Bill was there—three levels underground...

Drive carefully and steadily, he told himself as he switched off the radio and turned Steffi's nursery rhymes back on, singing along to 'One little, two little, three little ogres' and wondering why nursery rhymes, like most fairy-tales, were unnecessarily grim.

Steffi, however, loved it, and after they'd done monsters and goblins he had to turn off the next song and keep singing, coming up with other creatures like bun-yips and yetis that they could include in the song.

'Miss Bill, she sings this song too,' Dolores said, and Nick felt his stomach clench.

How stupid had he been to even consider Serena might want to be a mother to their child! Serena, who hadn't once cuddled her daughter, let alone sung her a song.

They stopped by a park and got out to let Steffi play awhile, Dolores buying sandwiches and fresh bottles of water, heating Steffi's bottle in a café across the road, promising Steffi a proper cooked meal once they reached home.

'No more of this bottled stuff,' she told the little girl, who didn't seem to mind what she ate any more than she objected to a two-thousand-kilometre car ride.

Dolores drove and he tried to sleep, but the closer they got to Willowby the more anxious he became. In the end he phoned Bob.

The tube was harder. It caught on things and bent the way she didn't want it to go, not that she could see where she *did* want it to go. She reached one arm as far forward as she could, scraping it, even through her overalls, against the jutting rock but needing to find the obstacle that lay ahead.

Loose dirt.

Dirt was easy.

Dig it out.

Glad she was wearing gloves, she dug and scraped, pulling the dirt back towards her body, tucking it under herself then digging and scraping again.

Behind her she could hear the anxiety building,

someone trying to push the tube further into her tunnel, although she wasn't ready for it.

She tried to explain the problem to the men back at the rock fall but as she had no earpiece she didn't know if she'd been heard. So she continued, digging, scraping, pulling back the dirt until finally the tube advanced, very slowly, guided by the wire and now her hand, which might be stuck in the hole for ever the way she was feeling now.

They were within four hours of home, late on the second day of their mammoth journey, when they heard that the eleven men, one seriously injured, would shortly be brought to the surface of the mine.

In an unemotional tone the reporter announced that rescue attempts were continuing for the three other miners.

'And that's all?' Nick demanded of the radio, because by now he knew, from Bob, that Bill was down that mine.

'She will be safe,' Dolores assured him. 'The one thing Bill is is sensible so she won't take any risks.'

'Oh, no?' Nick muttered, and drove on.

The tube went through.

Bill heard the shout of delight then felt it move beneath her as they tugged it further into their small area of dubious safety.

Now to get out so things could be fed through the tube. Water and eventually food going in, information about the situation in the tunnel coming out. The probe was good for communication but if the engineers in charge of the rescue needed a diagram of the area and some indication of the placement of the rock fall, the men could supply it.

She began to edge backwards, harder to do now because of the tube *and* the dirt she'd shifted back.

Harder to do because she was tired.

Nonsense! You've been a lot tireder than this on night duty and still kept focussed on your work.

She edged a little further, inching backwards, body cramped and aching, praying that any moment someone would grasp her boot and she'd know she'd made it.

Nick dropped Dolores at the apartment, carried up all their baggage, then, not bothering to return the hire car, drove straight to the mine.

Growing up in Willowby, with mines on the doorstep of the town, he knew exactly where Macaw was, and if he hadn't, the mass of emergency and private vehicles parked nearby would have told him. Daylight was fading as he pulled up outside the high wire fence but bright arc lights lit up the scene so it was like something out of a movie.

Or a nightmare.

Certain they wouldn't let him in, he stood by the gate and scoured the grim faces of the men by the site office for one he knew.

Dan de Groote!

He yelled the name and Dan turned, saw him waving from behind the fence and came towards him.

'Word was you were back in Sydney,' Dan said, looking none too happy to see him.

'I'm not, I'm here. Bill's down there, isn't she? Can I come in and wait?'

Dan waved his hand towards the crowds of people gathered outside the fence.

'I should let you in and not all of them—other relatives?'

'I *am* a doctor,' Nick reminded him. 'I could be helpful.'

Dan's glance towards the ambulances already within the perimeter fence told Nick what he was thinking, but in the end he nodded.

'Just wait there while I get you a tag and once you're in keep out of everyone's way, okay?'

Nick almost smiled because just so had Dan, the eldest of the boys, always treated him and Bill, letting them join in some wild game the 'big boys' were playing, as long as they kept out of the way.

She couldn't move.

The tube had somehow changed the dynamics of the little tunnel. The tube and the probe and the dirt.

Well, she had to move, to wiggle and wriggle and ease herself just a little, forget inches, they were old measurements, go for millimetres. A millimetre at a time—she could do it.

Tag hanging around his neck, Nick waited on the periphery of the crowd of sober, worried men near the mine office. Something had gone wrong, he could tell from their voices.

And now arrangements were being made for more men to go down below, Dan saying very loudly he was going, Nick, without thinking, stepping forward.

'I'll go with you.'

Dan threw him a hard look.

'You're claustrophobic, remember?' he said, 'besides not being trained. But you can make yourself useful as a doctor. We brought up the badly injured man first and the doctor we had here has gone with him to hospital. The rest of the eleven men we've rescued are coming up now. Go check them out.'

He pointed to where a large tent had been set up, close to where the ambulances were parked, and Nick, knowing Dan was right—an untrained person in this situation could bring risk to all the rescuers—went across to make himself useful.

'Someone else is trapped, one of the mine rescue people.'

He heard the whisper as he waited for his patients to arrive and knew, with cold certainty in his gut, that it was Bill.

And he hadn't told her he loved her.

Where that thought came from he had no idea, but he knew it was true. The mad dash from Sydney had been for love.

CHAPTER THIRTEEN

FINALLY ALL ELEVEN men were up, checked and reunited with their anxious families before being ferried to hospital for more comprehensive examinations and treatment.

Night had fallen, and an eerie silence hung over the complex. Nick edged his way back towards the site office where, he knew, the rescue was being co-ordinated, and found not Dan but Pete.

Nick heard an echo of Bill's voice—Dan and Pete, both members of the elite rescue team—the best of the best.

'I'm going down,' Pete said. 'Dan let me know you were here. You want to come?'

One look at Pete's face was enough to confirm that the rescuer in trouble was the boys' adored little sister, Bill.

And in bad trouble if Pete was here, too.

Nick didn't hesitate, taking the overalls Pete was holding and clambering into them as he followed the miner to an area behind the main buildings.

'You won't go soft on me?' Pete demanded as he handed Nick a helmet with a light attached. 'We're going down three levels.'

'I won't go soft on you,' Nick promised, and they started carefully down the ladder that led into what, to Nick, was like the very centre of the earth.

One shaft, another, then another, until finally voices and bright lights led them to where the fall blocked the three men from escape. In the bright lights three miners, stripped down to underwear, sweat gleaming from their skins, were carefully levering and shifting rocks from the base of the fall. A rescuer in full gear talked quietly to the trapped men through a communication probe, and a thinish, flexible tube that led up and over the rock fall told Nick exactly where Bill was trapped.

He couldn't think of how far underground he was, all he could do was concentrate on Bill, willing her free from her prison. Pete had joined the men digging while Dan and the second rescue team member talked about tubes and probes and the possibility that there'd been a slight movement in the rocks that had been enough to trap Bill in her narrow tunnel.

'Can you remove the tube?' Nick asked Dan, and they all stared at the dark hole above their heads, seeking inspiration. 'Would that help?'

'Who knows? The danger is that in moving it we might do more damage. She's okay, she's only about a metre from the trapped men, and although she must have lost her mike while she was wiggling around, she is talking to them and they're relaying information back to us. Apparently she had to dig away some dirt to get the tube through and she pushed it back underneath her as she dug. Now she's using her free hand to dig it out from underneath her and trying to edge backwards that way.'

Nick closed his eyes, trying to picture the situation,

shutting down the panic in his chest when he considered just who was stuck in that unbearable situation.

'Suction? Like a vacuum cleaner?' he said to Dan. 'Would it alter the dynamics and make things worse if we sucked some loose dirt and rubble away from up there?'

Dan considered the idea for a moment then walked away to talk to the men.

'We can't use the mine's ventilation suction,' Pete said, 'it'd be far too strong and could bring down more rock, but Nick's idea is worth a go—some kind of industrial vacuum cleaner that'll suck up dirt.'

The second rescuer sent a message to the operations room and within ten minutes a very clumsy-looking barrel vacuum cleaner was in Nick's hands.

But not for long!

'Sorry, mate,' Dan said, 'but you have to take a back seat on this one. We can't risk a further fall.'

The valiant little machine sucked, was emptied, sucked again, emptied again, until a yell of triumph went up from the man currently manning it—Bill's boots were in sight, edging gradually towards them.

He shouldn't be here.

He didn't belong.

But how could he be anywhere else?

Pete reached up as the boots came closer, talking to Bill now, easing her feet down onto footholds in the rocks, talking all the time. But it was Nick who pushed both Dan and Pete aside to catch her as she fell the last few feet to the ground, catch her and hold her, just hold her.

'You're the doc, you're supposed to be checking her

out,' Dan reminded him, but Nick's arms wouldn't un-clamp from around the woman he'd so nearly lost.

Eventually he climbed behind her up the first shaft, Bill recovering enough to tease him all the way about how at any moment the earth could come crashing down on them.

'Don't worry, when I heard about Macaw I thought it had,' he told her. 'I thought I'd lost you for ever with-out ever telling you I love you.'

'Telling me you love me?'

Bill's startled reply echoed down the shaft but hope-fully they were far enough up for it not to have been heard by the men still working below.

'Of course I love you. According to Serena I always have, I just hadn't realised it.'

Bill had reached the next level and waited until he emerged when, ignoring the miner standing guard there, she turned to hug him hard.

'Serena?' she asked.

'We'll work it out,' he assured her.

'Steffi?'

'We'll work that out too.'

Nick eased his arms from around her and looked into her dirt- and blood-streaked face.

'Preferably above ground,' he reminded her, and she led him to the next shaft and began to climb.

'When did you get here?' she asked, and it took most of that climb to explain their mad drive north.

The third shaft was easier, the light from above re-assuring Nick that the real world still existed. But Bill was tiring fast, so he climbed closer to her, trying to take some of her weight off her arms and legs, half car-rying her when they finally reached the top and anxious helpers hauled out first Bill then helped him clamber up and stand upright.

Paramedics had already put Bill onto a stretcher and as they wheeled her to the makeshift emergency room, he walked beside her, holding her hand, not caring what anyone thought.

Apart from a multitude of scratches, torn nails and fingers from her digging, and red patches that would eventually be bruises, she was fine.

'Nothing a good hot shower won't cure,' he told her, when he'd finished what he'd tried to make a professional examination, although his heart went into overdrive when he remembered the danger she'd been in.

'Take me home,' she said quietly, and Nick was only too happy to oblige.

She was quiet in the car, sitting with one hand on his knee, and he knew the stress of her entrapment must be catching up with her.

Except that when she spoke, it was to ask what she'd asked earlier.

'Serena?'

He shrugged.

'I don't know,' he said, 'I really don't. All I know is that I'd be living a lie if I settled with her, loving you as I do. I had thought it was the right thing to do for Steffi, but now I realise it would be unfair to everyone. Somehow we've got to come to some agreement over Steffi without her becoming the rope in a tug-of-war. But all that can wait. You're safe and you probably need some sleep and I definitely need some sleep, and tomorrow, as the wise men say, is another day.'

'I think we might be at tomorrow already,' Bill reminded him, and she moved the hand that lay on his knee, giving him a little squeeze that brought him more joy, right then, than a kiss.

He took her back to her own apartment, where he helped her out of her clothes, showered her gently, applied antiseptic lotion to the scratches and put dressings on her hands, then slid a big T-shirt over her head and tucked her into bed.

'I'll take your spare key so Dolores can bring you some food,' he told her, bending to kiss her on the lips.

She slid her arms around his neck.

'You're not staying?' she whispered. 'I thought you'd wanted us to be here alone? That night at the yacht club?'

'No, I'm not staying and, yes, I do want us to be alone, but not now, not like this, my love,' he responded, kissing her again, but gently still. 'You need to sleep and then you need to think about where *you* want to go in this situation. It might be hard, Bill, if I have to fight Serena because there's no way I'm giving up Steffi. If that happens, you'll be caught in the crossfire.'

She cupped his face in her palms.

'And if I said I didn't care—that however bad things get they couldn't be worse than life without you?' she asked him. 'If I said I loved you?'

His heart was behaving badly again and it was only with a mammoth effort of will that he eased away from her, tucked the sheet around her and kissed her one more time, this time a goodnight kiss but not goodbye...

Bill woke, stiff and more than a little sore but with a sense of well-being in spite of her physical state. She examined her surroundings as she considered this state and slowly memory returned—Nick had kissed her goodnight—and she had to smile.

Although...

Might have to fight Serena—you'll be caught in the crossfire—Steffi rope in tug-of-war...

Memories of before the kiss dampened the sense of well-being.

It was all very well being gung-ho about fighting side by side with Nick so he could keep Steffi, but what if they lost?

What would it do to Nick?

Thinking of that was bad enough, but she knew she was only throwing that around in her head to stop herself thinking of the big one.

What would it do to her?

Okay, so she already loved Steffi, but at a distance— a little closer than her nephews and nieces but still as an outsider in her heart. But if she married Nick—and that had seemed to be the gist of things last night—and having mother 'rights' so to speak, Bill knew damn well her love for the little girl would send its roots deep into her heart.

And *then* to lose her?

From being ready to leap out of bed, shower, and rush up to see Nick and Steffi, Bill indulged in a tiny whimper of self-pity and stuck her head under the pillow.

Two minutes later she realised just how pathetic her behaviour was. She didn't do the leap-from-bed thing but she did drag her body up and out into the shower, where all her scrapes were red and sore and her bruises coming out nicely.

She stood under the steaming water until it started to

get cold—Bob must have put in cheap water heaters—
then she dried her herself, rubbed at her hair, carefully
dressed herself—whimpering occasionally at the pain of
movement or when she dragged clothing over an extra
sore spot—then made her way up to Nick's apartment.

It was Nick she had to consider in this business—
Nick her friend, Nick the man she loved and, if memory
served correctly, Nick who loved her back.

Nick who'd overcome his very real claustrophobia
to come down a mine to help rescue her.

And she was going to leave him to battle Serena on
his own?

Not stand beside him because of some wimpish fear
of being hurt?

She rang the bell of his apartment but when he appeared, Steffi in his arms, she felt again that dreaded
fear of loss.

Nick looped his arm around her and drew her inside,
scolding quietly all the time.

'You should have stayed in bed. Dolores is making some chicken soup for you. Have you had enough
sleep? How are your cuts and scratches? I'll have to have
a look, put something on them. Come and sit down.'

The words flowed over Bill like balm, but although
they soothed it was the way Steffi's fingers caught at
her hair that hurt more than scratches.

Bill eased away and sank down into an armchair,
staring at a mess of Steffi's toys on the living-room
floor. Nick set the little girl down and she toddled off
into the kitchen.

'She's walking properly now,' Bill said, and the mix
of happiness and dread made her voice crack.

Nick came and sat on the arm of her chair, tangling

his fingers in her still-damp hair the way his daughter had.

'Tell me,' he commanded, and somehow Bill did, pouring out her doubts and fears.

'It hurt so much, losing the baby, Nick,' she said, doing pathetic again, 'that now, twelve months later, I'm only barely over it. I just don't know if I could go through that again—if I'd find the courage a second time around.'

Nick lifted her out of the chair, and sat down in it with her on his knee.

'I can't pretend there's not a chance,' he told her, his lips pressing kisses on her neck by way of punctuation. 'But do we throw away the joy and happiness we could have now—right now—because of what might happen in the future?

'By some miracle we've found each other in a way we never expected to—we've loved each other for so long, but this love is different, special and all the more powerful because of the love that was already there. So it might not move mountains, but with you by my side—and now I've been down to Level Three in a mine—I'd give it a damn good try.'

He turned her enough to kiss her properly now and Bill felt all his conviction—and all his love, *their* love—in that long, deep, probing kiss.

Eventually, she kissed him back, telling him without words that she agreed.

Or thought she did.

A long time later he lifted his head and looked down into her face.

'I would understand if you decided to run for your

life—to head off to deepest, darkest somewhere to get away from this.'

The slight tremor in his voice told her he meant every word, and it was that tremor that restored her courage.

'When you've gone down to Level Three for me?' she teased softly, then *she* kissed *him*.

CHAPTER FOURTEEN

'So, what happened in Sydney?'

Such a simple question, Nick thought as Bill clambered off his lap and settled on the floor close to his legs, looking up at him with such trust and love and hope he found it hard to talk.

Let alone explain.

'I've no idea,' he admitted honestly. 'Well, to a certain extent I can describe the visit, but the underlying currents are beyond me.'

He hesitated.

How could he tell Bill about Serena's attitude without being disloyal to his daughter's mother or portraying her as cold and heartless, which he knew for a fact she wasn't?

'Start when you arrived,' Bill suggested, resting her head on his knee so she was no longer looking up at him.

Which somehow made it easier...

'It was weird, Bill. For a start, she barely acknowledged Steffi's existence. Alex was there and he was delighted to see Stef and she was obviously just as pleased to see him, but Serena...'

Another pause as he tried to recall their arrival, but

the days had blended into each other and the bit he had to get out wasn't getting any easier.

'I don't know why,' he said, still hesitant, 'but for some reason she had taken if for granted we'd get back together—physically. I think I might have told you that. It didn't make sense, especially when she didn't seem to care about Steffi at all and got downright angry when Alex suggested he photograph Steffi again.'

Having got that out, he lapsed into silence because he couldn't think of any more words to say.

Bill, resting against his legs, reached up one hand to grasp one of his and they sat in silence for a while until finally she stood up and perched on the arm of the chair.

'If you think back to when she was persuaded by Alex to keep the baby so he could photograph her, at that stage she was determined to give Steffi up for adoption as soon as she was born, so I would imagine, during her pregnancy, she was determined not to get emotionally attached to the child she was carrying.'

'Hmm,' was all Nick could add to that suggestion, although it did make a kind of sense. 'But after that, when she *did* keep Steffi?'

'Again it was for Alex. She's been his favourite model for ever, his muse, as you called her, and suddenly here's this interloper capturing his attention. You said she got angry when he wanted to photograph Steffi here—maybe it's nothing more than Serena's own insecurity. Maybe that's why she wanted you back again, so she'd have the security of someone special in her life. From what I've read of Alex, he's getting old, and a model's working life doesn't last for ever, so…'

Nick reached up so he could pull Bill's head down to his and kiss her.

'You realise you're making excuses for a woman you barely know, and what you do know about her must make your teeth itch.'

Bill grinned at him and he felt his heart swoop around his chest in a great burst of love.

'I'm not really. I've never understood other people's relationships and I don't try, but I would imagine there's huge insecurity in any model's life—are my looks going, am I getting fat, will I get the top jobs this year? Possibly having Steffi around only added to it. If you think about Serena's childhood, she barely stopped working to *be* a child, so she's probably at a loss as to what to do with one.'

'You're probably right,' he told her, and kissed her again, because not only was she beautiful, and bright, and a wonderful woman, but she was kind, and compassionate, and understanding—and he wanted to kiss her anyway.

'Do you think she'll fight for Steffi?'

So they were back there again—back in doubtful land, with Bill remembering the pain of loss.

'I can't promise that she won't,' he said.

Now, Bill thought to herself. Now's the time to commit to Nick.

'Of course you can't,' she said, 'but I can promise that, whatever happens, I'll be with you every step of the way—with both of you.'

Nick stood up and pulled her into his arms again, holding her close, not kissing her, just holding her, and Bill knew that everything would be all right. Somehow they would get through whatever the future might hold because their love was strong enough to—

Well, to move mountains!

'Marry me,' he whispered in her ear, just as Steffi came toddling back, her high-pitched 'Beee!' making them spring fairly guiltily apart.

The day, which had begun underground about a million years ago, was finally drawing to a close. With Steffi in bed, and Dolores visiting her family for the last few days of the leave Nick had taken, he and Bill were alone on the deck, lights out, looking out to sea, sipping hot chocolate with marshmallows in it because it had been that kind of day.

'You didn't answer my proposal,' Nick complained when, his drink finished, he set the cup down and took Bill's hand in both of his.

'What proposal?' she demanded, turning to face him. In the dim light reflecting up from the marina her hair was a dark cloud around her pale face, her eyes nothing more than deep shadows.

'My proposal in the living room'

'In the living room?'

He could practically hear the gears turning in her head and wondered how far he could push her before she exploded into anger.

'I asked you something,' he reminded her, telling himself that teasing her was only getting a little of his own back for his panicked agony of the rescue mission.

'You *did* not!'

Good, she was angry now and he loved an angry Bill. Once she'd let fly at him he could take her in his arms and feel the tension in her body then feel it ease as he held and kissed her, eventually feeling it turn to a different kind of tension...

And why the hell was he wasting time teasing her like this when he could be holding her, kissing her right now?

He stood up and pulled her out of the chair, wrapping his arms around her just as he'd known he would.

'I said, marry me, remember?' he whispered as he brushed the hair back from her ear to kiss her in the hollow just below it. 'Steffi came in and you didn't answer and now it's too late because I'm taking no answer as a yes and I'm going to kiss the breath out of you.'

'Starting here,' he added, his mouth taking possession of hers.

'Like this,' he murmured, sliding his tongue between her lips...

Random questions flashed through Bill's head. Was this okay? Hadn't it been too sudden? Was it just Steffi that had brought them together? This was Nick, but was this love?

She heard a faint moan and thought it might have been hers, then her mind went blank and she gave in to sensation—to the warmth in her blood, the fire along her nerves, the prickly expectation on her skin and the ache of desire deep within her body.

All this from a kiss?

All this and more because kissing Nick was like nothing she'd ever experienced before, like nothing anyone in the universe could possibly have experienced because otherwise they'd all be doing it right now...

'Bed?'

She heard the word but was still grasping for its meaning, too lost in sensation to be thinking straight.

Had she hesitated too long that Nick released his hold on her, just slightly, so he could look down into her face.

'Too soon?'

She smiled, and shrugged, and felt the heat that told her she was blushing like a schoolgirl.

'No—yes—oh, I don't know.'

'I do,' he whispered, and kissed her once again, so gently, so thoroughly, so beautifully she had an urge to cry—again! 'It's been a very long and enormously emotional day, one way and another, so for tonight we shall be abstinent. In fact, how soon can you organise a wedding? We could stay abstinent till then, get a few days off somewhere, with Dolores minding Steffi, and stay in bed the entire time, room service providing enough in the way of food to keep up our strength.'

Bill smiled at him—at her friend Nick, trying, as always, to do the right thing. She rested her hand on his cheek and said, 'Or we could go to bed tomorrow night...'

EPILOGUE

GIVEN THE SIZE of Bill's family, they'd decided to hold Steffi's second birthday party in a park. Balloons hung from trees, a marquee festooned with ribbons provided shade and shelter should it be necessary, and twenty-three small boys and girls, all dressed, more or less, as bears were rioting on the grass.

'Do we have to do this party thing every birthday?' Nick demanded, coming to sit beside his wife, who was settled on a folding chair in the shade of a tree, watching three of her brothers trying to organise a pin-the-tail-on-the-donkey game with very little success.

Katie, the eldest of the de Groote grandchildren, had adopted Steffi from their first meeting, and she was organising some of the smaller ones in some game that involved standing up then falling over, the little ones screaming with glee.

'I think every second year will be enough,' Bill told him, 'but then on the off years this one will probably need a party, so get used to it.'

Nick reached over to pat the very large bulge of his wife's stomach.

'If you got this guy out today or tomorrow then we

could combine the parties, considering Steffi's real birthday isn't until tomorrow.'

'Yes, but would it be fair?'

She was actually frowning over the fairness of combined birthday parties for her children and Nick felt again a gust of love so strong it nearly struck him down. He had thought that after a year of marriage this might stop happening, but although he loved Bill all the time—well ninety-nine point nine per cent of the time as she could still be aggravating—these gusts of love still came out of nowhere, leaving him shaken at the thought that this might never have happened—that they might never have got together in this way, just gone on being friends and lost the magical, rewarding, cosmic wonder that was their love.

Steffi, with Katie's help, was blowing out the candles on the bear birthday cake when Bill felt the first contraction.

Hmm, the doctor had said any day now, although she still had a fortnight to go.

Ignoring it, she helped cut the bear into small sections and handed around plates of gooey chocolate cake.

The second contraction suggested things might be getting serious. Could she really have the baby on Steffi's birthday?

This time last year she'd been preparing to get married—they'd decided their daughter's birthday was as good a day as any.

Preparing to marry Nick—her BFF.

It still seemed surreal, yet sometimes when she caught an unexpected glimpse of him and her insides turned upside down, she knew that it was real—somehow they'd moved from friends to lovers, from friend-

ship to passion so hard and hot she could feel herself
blushing right now as she thought about it.

She'd read somewhere once that love was all-encompassing, and as the third contraction tightened her belly,
Bill looked around at all her family, at Gran, wearing bear ears on her head, various de Grootes in fancy
dress, Steffi the cutest bear of all, theirs now Serena had
agreed they have custody, Dolores, on standby for when
Bill went into hospital. Yes, love *was* all-encompassing!

Nick came and stood beside her, his arm coming to
rest around her shoulders.

'Not to worry you,' she said quietly, 'but you might
drop me off at the hospital on your way back to the
apartment.'

He turned to look at her, his face going pale under
his tan.

'You're serious?'

She smiled and with difficulty got close enough to
kiss him on the lips.

'Of course! I'm a nurse, remember, I know these
things.'

'But shouldn't you be sitting—or lying down—or
doing *something*?'

'I am, I'm counting the minutes between contractions
and you've been to all the pre-natal classes, you know
I can stand up and move around as much as I like all
through the birth if I want to. Right now I want to watch
everyone enjoying themselves, but you might speak to
Dolores and tell her we'll need her to move in tonight.'

Nick stared at her.

'You're for real?'

She had to laugh.

'Nick, you knew this was coming. You said yourself

today or tomorrow would be good. Surely you're not going to go to pieces on me now?'

He wasn't, of course!

He was a doctor, he knew about this stuff, it was just that his brain had stopped working and his legs were none too steady, and he wasn't sure that he could handle having two children—could he love them equally, could he ever love another child as much as he loved Steffi?—and then there was Bill, and he didn't know that he could go through seeing her in pain like he'd seen other women during labour, and—

'Nick!'

Bill's voice brought him out of his funk.

Well, almost.

'Go and talk to Dolores, ask Kirsten if she'd mind organising the clean-up here at the park, then we'll put Steffi and all the presents in the car, you can drop me at the hospital, then when Dolores gets to the apartment you can come back to the hospital.'

He stared at her.

'And bring my bag—the one that's packed. We've been through this.'

Nick stared at her some more, saw her smile and knew she knew exactly what he was thinking.

She kissed him once again, although he felt the wince of pain she gave as another contraction grabbed her body.

'We'll be fine,' she promised him. 'You'll love this baby differently from Steffi but still love him just as much. Love is the one thing we've got plenty of. And I won't die in childbirth and you won't faint, watching it.'

She looked at him again and added, 'Now, was there anything else?'

He shook his head and took her in his arms.

'Except to tell you that I love you, Mrs Grant,' he said, his voice so husky he wondered if she'd heard the words.

'That's good,' Bill told him. 'Now go and talk to Kirsten and Dolores and find Steffi and the presents and—'

Nick cut off the instructions with another kiss and when Bill kissed him back he knew she was right, and that this new baby he and Bill had made would be every bit as special as Steffi, and—

Well, he couldn't really remember all the other things he'd been worrying about.

Stuart Alexander Grant, weighing in at a splendid three point eight kilos, arrived on his sister's birthday, much to everyone's delight. Holding him in his arms, looking down into his red, downy face, Nick felt again that rush of pure, unadulterated love he'd felt when he'd first held Steffi.

'We'll be right, mate,' he said to his son, then looked up into the radiance of Bill's smile, at Steffi cuddled up to Bill on the bed, her little fist holding tightly to Bill's curls, and he knew they'd all be right—his family!

* * * * *

Mills & Boon® Hardback

May 2013

ROMANCE

A Rich Man's Whim	Lynne Graham
A Price Worth Paying?	Trish Morey
A Touch of Notoriety	Carole Mortimer
The Secret Casella Baby	Cathy Williams
Maid for Montero	Kim Lawrence
Captive in his Castle	Chantelle Shaw
Heir to a Dark Inheritance	Maisey Yates
A Legacy of Secrets	Carol Marinelli
Her Deal with the Devil	Nicola Marsh
One More Sleepless Night	Lucy King
A Father for Her Triplets	Susan Meier
The Matchmaker's Happy Ending	Shirley Jump
Second Chance with the Rebel	Cara Colter
First Comes Baby...	Michelle Douglas
Anything but Vanilla...	Liz Fielding
It was Only a Kiss	Joss Wood
Return of the Rebel Doctor	Joanna Neil
One Baby Step at a Time	Meredith Webber

MEDICAL

NYC Angels: Flirting with Danger	Tina Beckett
NYC Angels: Tempting Nurse Scarlet	Wendy S. Marcus
One Life Changing Moment	Lucy Clark
P.S. You're a Daddy!	Dianne Drake

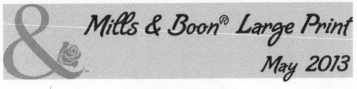

Mills & Boon® Large Print

May 2013

ROMANCE

Beholden to the Throne	Carol Marinelli
The Petrelli Heir	Kim Lawrence
Her Little White Lie	Maisey Yates
Her Shameful Secret	Susanna Carr
The Incorrigible Playboy	Emma Darcy
No Longer Forbidden?	Dani Collins
The Enigmatic Greek	Catherine George
The Heir's Proposal	Raye Morgan
The Soldier's Sweetheart	Soraya Lane
The Billionaire's Fair Lady	Barbara Wallace
A Bride for the Maverick Millionaire	Marion Lennox

HISTORICAL

Some Like to Shock	Carole Mortimer
Forbidden Jewel of India	Louise Allen
The Caged Countess	Joanna Fulford
Captive of the Border Lord	Blythe Gifford
Behind the Rake's Wicked Wager	Sarah Mallory

MEDICAL

Maybe This Christmas…?	Alison Roberts
A Doctor, A Fling & A Wedding Ring	Fiona McArthur
Dr Chandler's Sleeping Beauty	Melanie Milburne
Her Christmas Eve Diamond	Scarlet Wilson
Newborn Baby For Christmas	Fiona Lowe
The War Hero's Locked-Away Heart	Louisa George

Mills & Boon® Hardback

June 2013

ROMANCE

The Sheikh's Prize	Lynne Graham
Forgiven but not Forgotten?	Abby Green
His Final Bargain	Melanie Milburne
A Throne for the Taking	Kate Walker
Diamond in the Desert	Susan Stephens
A Greek Escape	Elizabeth Power
Princess in the Iron Mask	Victoria Parker
An Invitation to Sin	Sarah Morgan
Too Close for Comfort	Heidi Rice
The Right Mr Wrong	Natalie Anderson
The Making of a Princess	Teresa Carpenter
Marriage for Her Baby	Raye Morgan
The Man Behind the Pinstripes	Melissa McClone
Falling for the Rebel Falcon	Lucy Gordon
Secrets & Saris	Shoma Narayanan
The First Crush Is the Deepest	Nina Harrington
One Night She Would Never Forget	Amy Andrews
When the Cameras Stop Rolling...	Connie Cox

MEDICAL

NYC Angels: Making the Surgeon Smile	Lynne Marshall
NYC Angels: An Explosive Reunion	Alison Roberts
The Secret in His Heart	Caroline Anderson
The ER's Newest Dad	Janice Lynn

Mills & Boon® Large Print

June 2013

ROMANCE

Sold to the Enemy	Sarah Morgan
Uncovering the Silveri Secret	Melanie Milburne
Bartering Her Innocence	Trish Morey
Dealing Her Final Card	Jennie Lucas
In the Heat of the Spotlight	Kate Hewitt
No More Sweet Surrender	Caitlin Crews
Pride After Her Fall	Lucy Ellis
Her Rocky Mountain Protector	Patricia Thayer
The Billionaire's Baby SOS	Susan Meier
Baby out of the Blue	Rebecca Winters
Ballroom to Bride and Groom	Kate Hardy

HISTORICAL

Never Trust a Rake	Annie Burrows
Dicing with the Dangerous Lord	Margaret McPhee
Haunted by the Earl's Touch	Ann Lethbridge
The Last de Burgh	Deborah Simmons
A Daring Liaison	Gail Ranstrom

MEDICAL

From Christmas to Eternity	Caroline Anderson
Her Little Spanish Secret	Laura Iding
Christmas with Dr Delicious	Sue MacKay
One Night That Changed Everything	Tina Beckett
Christmas Where She Belongs	Meredith Webber
His Bride in Paradise	Joanna Neil

0513 GEN STD LP